THE METAMORPHOSIS
DIE·VERWANDLUNG

THE METAMORPHOSIS
DIE VERWANDLUNG

FRANZ KAFKA

TRANSLATION BY WILLA AND EDWIN MUIR

SCHOCKEN BOOKS • NEW YORK

First SCHOCKEN PAPERBACK edition 1968
Ninth Printing, 1974

Copyright 1935 by Schocken Verlag, Berlin
Copyright © 1946, 1948 by Schocken Books Inc., New York
Library of Congress Catalog Card No. HE 68–151
Manufactured in the United States of America

THE METAMORPHOSIS
DIE VERWANDLUNG

Die Verwandlung

I

ALS GREGOR SAMSA eines Morgens aus unruhigen Träumen
erwachte, fand er sich in seinem Bett zu einem ungeheuren
Ungeziefer verwandelt. Er lag auf seinem panzerartig har-
ten Rücken und sah, wenn er den Kopf ein wenig hob,
seinen gewölbten, braunen, von bogenförmigen Verstei-
fungen geteilten Bauch, auf dessen Höhe sich die Bett-
decke, zum gänzlichen Niedergleiten bereit, kaum noch
erhalten konnte. Seine vielen, im Vergleich zu seinem
sonstigen Umfang kläglich dünnen Beine flimmerten ihm
hilflos vor den Augen.

Was ist mit mir geschehen? dachte er. Es war kein
Traum. Sein Zimmer, ein richtiges, nur etwas zu kleines
Menschenzimmer, lag ruhig zwischen den vier wohlbekann-
ten Wänden. Über dem Tisch, auf dem eine auseinander-
gepackte Musterkollektion von Tuchwaren ausgebreitet
war — Samsa war Reisender —, hing das Bild, das er vor
kurzem aus einer illustrierten Zeitschrift ausgeschnitten
und in einem hübschen, vergoldeten Rahmen untergebracht
hatte. Es stellte eine Dame dar, die, mit einem Pelzhut und
einer Pelzboa versehen, aufrecht dasass und einen schweren
Pelzmuff, in dem ihr ganzer Unterarm verschwunden war,
dem Beschauer entgegenhob.

Gregors Blick richtete sich dann zum Fenster, und das
trübe Wetter — man hörte Regentropfen auf das Fenster-
blech aufschlagen — machte ihn ganz melancholisch. Wie
wäre es, wenn ich noch ein wenig weiterschliefe und alle
Narrheiten vergässe, dachte er, aber das war gänzlich un-

The Metamorphosis

1

As GREGOR SAMSA awoke one morning from uneasy dreams he found himself transformed in his bed into a gigantic insect. He was lying on his hard, as it were armor-plated, back and when he lifted his head a little he could see his dome-like brown belly divided into stiff arched segments on top of which the bed quilt could hardly keep in position and was about to slide off completely. His numerous legs, which were pitifully thin compared to the rest of his bulk, waved helplessly before his eyes.

What has happened to me? he thought. It was no dream. His room, a regular human bedroom, only rather too small, lay quiet between the four familiar walls. Above the table on which a collection of cloth samples was unpacked and spread out—Samsa was a commercial traveler—hung the picture which he had recently cut out of an illustrated magazine and put into a pretty gilt frame. It showed a lady, with a fur cap on and a fur stole, sitting upright and holding out to the spectator a huge fur muff into which the whole of her forearm had vanished!

Gregor's eyes turned next to the window, and the overcast sky—one could hear rain drops beating on the window gutter—made him quite melancholy. What about sleeping a little longer and forgetting all this nonsense, he thought, but it could not be done, for he was accus-

durchführbar, denn er war gewöhnt, auf der rechten Seite
zu schlafen, konnte sich aber in seinem gegenwärtigen
Zustand nicht in diese Lage bringen. Mit welcher Kraft
er sich auch auf die rechte Seite warf, immer wieder schau-
kelte er in die Rückenlage zurück. Er versuchte es wohl
hundertmal, schloss die Augen, um die zappelnden Beine
nicht sehen zu müssen, und liess erst ab, als er in der Seite
einen noch nie gefühlten, leichten, dumpfen Schmerz zu
fühlen begann.

Ach Gott, dachte er, was für einen anstrengenden Beruf
habe ich gewählt! Tag aus, Tag ein auf der Reise. Die
geschäftlichen Aufregungen sind viel grösser, als im eigentlichen Geschäft zu Hause, und ausserdem ist mir noch diese
Plage des Reisens auferlegt, die Sorgen um die Zugan-
schlüsse, das unregelmässige, schlechte Essen, ein immer
wechselnder, nie andauernder, nie herzlich werdender
menschlicher Verkehr. Der Teufel soll das alles holen! Er
fühlte ein leichtes Jucken oben auf dem Bauch; schob
sich auf dem Rücken langsam näher zum Bettpfosten,
um den Kopf besser heben zu können; fand die juckende
Stelle, die mit lauter kleinen weissen Pünktchen besetzt war,
die er nicht zu beurteilen verstand; und wollte mit einem
Bein die Stelle betasten, zog es aber gleich zurück, denn
bei der Berührung umwehten ihn Kälteschauer.

Er glitt wieder in seine frühere Lage zurück. Dies früh-
zeitige Aufstehen, dachte er, macht einen ganz blödsinnig.
Der Mensch muss seinen Schlaf haben. Andere Reisende
leben wie Haremsfrauen. Wenn ich zum Beispiel im Laufe
des Vormittags ins Gasthaus zurückgehe, um die erlangten
Aufträge zu überschreiben, sitzen diese Herren erst beim
Frühstück. Das sollte ich bei meinem Chef versuchen; ich
würde auf der Stelle hinausfliegen. Wer weiss übrigens,
ob das nicht sehr gut für mich wäre. Wenn ich mich nicht
wegen meiner Eltern zurückhielte, ich hätte längst ge-
kündigt, ich wäre vor den Chef hingetreten und hätte ihm
meine Meinung von Grund des Herzens aus gesagt. Vom
Pult hätte er fallen müssen! Es ist auch eine sonderbare

tomed to sleep on his right side and in his present condition he could not turn himself over. However violently
he forced himself towards his right side he always rolled
on to his back again. He tried it at least a hundred times,
shutting his eyes to keep from seeing his struggling legs,
and only desisted when he began to feel in his side a
faint dull ache he had never experienced before.

Oh God, he thought, what an exhausting job I've
picked on! Traveling about day in, day out. It's much
more irritating work than doing the actual business in
the office, and on top of that there's the trouble of
constant traveling, of worrying about train connections,
the bad and irregular meals, casual acquaintances that
are always new and never become intimate friends. The
devil take it all! He felt a slight itching up on his belly;
slowly pushed himself on his back nearer to the top of
the bed so that he could lift his head more easily;
identified the itching place which was surrounded by
many small white spots the nature of which he could
not understand and made to touch it with a leg, but
drew the leg back immediately, for the contact made a
cold shiver run through him.

He slid down again into his former position. This
getting up early, he thought, makes one quite stupid. A
man needs his sleep. Other commercials live like harem
women. For instance, when I come back to the hotel of a
morning to write up the orders I've got, these others are
only sitting down to breakfast. Let me just try that with
my chief; I'd be sacked on the spot. Anyhow, that might
be quite a good thing for me, who can tell? If I didn't
have to hold my hand because of my parents I'd have
given notice long ago, I'd have gone to the chief and
told him exactly what I think of him. That would knock
him endways from his desk! It's a queer way of doing,
too, this sitting on high at a desk and talking down to

Art, sich auf das Pult zu setzen und von der Höhe herab
mit dem Angestellten zu reden, der überdies wegen der
Schwerhörigkeit des Chefs ganz nahe herantreten muss.
Nun, die Hoffnung ist noch nicht gänzlich aufgegeben;
habe ich einmal das Geld beisammen, um die Schuld der
Eltern an ihn abzuzahlen — es dürfte noch fünf bis sechs
Jahre dauern —, mache ich die Sache unbedingt. Dann
wird der grosse Schnitt gemacht. Vorläufig allerdings muss
ich aufstehen, denn mein Zug fährt um fünf.

Und er sah zur Weckuhr hinüber, die auf dem Kasten
tickte. Himmlischer Vater! dachte er. Es war halb sieben
Uhr, und die Zeiger gingen ruhig vorwärts, es war sogar
halb vorüber, es näherte sich schon dreiviertel. Sollte der
Wecker nicht geläutet haben? Man sah vom Bett aus, dass
er auf vier Uhr richtig eingestellt war; gewiss hatte er
auch geläutet. Ja, aber war es möglich, dieses möbelerschüt-
ternde Läuten ruhig zu verschlafen? Nun, ruhig hatte er
ja nicht geschlafen, aber wahrscheinlich desto fester. Was
aber sollte er jetzt tun? Der nächste Zug ging um sieben
Uhr; um den einzuholen, hätte er sich unsinnig beeilen
müssen, und die Kollektion war noch nicht eingepackt,
und er selbst fühlte sich durchaus nicht besonders frisch
und beweglich. Und selbst wenn er den Zug einholte, ein
Donnerwetter des Chefs war nicht zu vermeiden, denn der
Geschäftsdiener hatte beim Fünfuhrzug gewartet und die
Meldung von seiner Versäumnis längst erstattet. Er war
eine Kreatur des Chefs, ohne Rückgrat und Verstand. Wie
nun, wenn er sich krank meldete? Das wäre aber äusserst
peinlich und verdächtig, denn Gregor war während seines
fünfjährigen Dienstes noch nicht einmal krank gewesen.
Gewiss würde der Chef mit dem Krankenkassenarzt kommen, würde den Eltern wegen des faulen Sohnes Vorwürfe
machen und alle Einwände durch den Hinweis auf den
Krankenkassenarzt abschneiden, für den es ja überhaupt
nur ganz gesunde, aber arbeitsscheue Menschen gibt. Und
hätte er übrigens in diesem Falle so ganz unrecht? Gregor
fühlte sich tatsächlich, abgesehen von einer nach dem

employees, especially when they have to come quite near because the chief is hard of hearing. Well, there's still hope; once I've saved enough money to pay back my parents' debts to him—that should take another five or six years—I'll do it without fail. I'll cut myself completely loose then. For the moment, though, I'd better get up, since my train goes at five.

He looked at the alarm clock ticking on the chest. Heavenly Father! he thought. It was half-past six o'clock and the hands were quietly moving on, it was even past the half-hour, it was getting on toward a quarter to seven. Had the alarm clock not gone off? From the bed one could see that it had been properly set for four o'clock; of course it must have gone off. Yes, but was it possible to sleep quietly through that ear-splitting noise? Well, he had not slept quietly, yet apparently all the more soundly for that. But what was he to do now? The next train went at seven o'clock; to catch that he would need to hurry like mad and his samples weren't even packed up, and he himself wasn't feeling particularly fresh and active. And even if he did catch the train he wouldn't avoid a row with the chief, since the firm's porter would have been waiting for the five o'clock train and would have long since reported his failure to turn up. The porter was a creature of the chief's, spineless and stupid. Well, supposing he were to say he was sick? But that would be most unpleasant and would look suspicious, since during his five years' employment he had not been ill once. The chief himself would be sure to come with the sick-insurance doctor, would reproach his parents with their son's laziness and would cut all excuses short by referring to the insurance doctor, who of course regarded all mankind as perfectly healthy malingerers. And would he be so far wrong on this occasion? Gregor really felt quite well, apart from a

langen Schlaf wirklich überflüssigen Schläfrigkeit, ganz wohl und hatte sogar einen besonders kräftigen Hunger.

Als er dies alles in grösster Eile überlegte, ohne sich entschliessen zu können, das Bett zu verlassen — gerade schlug der Wecker dreiviertel sieben —, klopfte es vorsichtig an die Tür am Kopfende seines Bettes. "Gregor," rief es — es war die Mutter —, "es ist dreiviertel sieben. Wolltest du nicht wegfahren?" Die sanfte Stimme! Gregor erschrak, als er seine antwortende Stimme hörte, die wohl unverkennbar seine frühere war, in die sich aber, wie von unten her, ein nicht zu unterdrückendes, schmerzliches Piepsen mischte, das die Worte förmlich nur im ersten Augenblick in ihrer Deutlichkeit beliess, um sie im Nachklang derart zu zerstören, dass man nicht wusste, ob man recht gehört hatte. Gregor hatte ausführlich antworten und alles erklären wollen, beschränkte sich aber bei diesen Umständen darauf, zu sagen: "Ja, ja, danke, Mutter, ich stehe schon auf." Infolge der Holztür war die Veränderung in Gregors Stimme draussen wohl nicht zu merken, denn die Mutter beruhigte sich mit dieser Erklärung und schlürfte davon. Aber durch das kleine Gespräch waren die anderen Familienmitglieder darauf aufmerksam geworden, dass Gregor wider Erwarten noch zu Hause war, und schon klopfte an der einen Seitentür der Vater, schwach, aber mit der Faust. "Gregor, Gregor," rief er, "was ist denn?" Und nach einer kleinen Weile mahnte er nochmals mit tieferer Stimme: "Gregor! Gregor!" An der anderen Seitentür aber klagte leise die Schwester: "Gregor? Ist dir nicht wohl? Brauchst du etwas?" Nach beiden Seiten hin antwortete Gregor: "Bin schon fertig", und bemühte sich, durch die sorgfältigste Aussprache und durch Einschaltung von langen Pausen zwischen den einzelnen Worten seiner Stimme alles Auffallende zu nehmen. Der Vater kehrte auch zu seinem Frühstück zurück, die Schwester aber flüsterte: "Gregor, mach auf, ich beschwöre dich." Gregor aber dachte gar nicht daran aufzumachen, sondern lobte die vom Reisen

drowsiness that was utterly superfluous after such a long sleep, and he was even unusually hungry.

As all this was running through his mind at top speed without his being able to decide to leave his bed—the alarm clock had just struck a quarter to seven—there came a cautious tap at the door behind the head of his bed. "Gregor," said a voice—it was his mother's—"it's a quarter to seven. Hadn't you a train to catch?" That gentle voice! Gregor had a shock as he heard his own voice answering hers, unmistakably his own voice, it was true, but with a persistent horrible twittering squeak behind it like an undertone, that left the words in their clear shape only for the first moment and then rose up reverberating round them to destroy their sense, so that one could not be sure one had heard them rightly. Gregor wanted to answer at length and explain everything, but in the circumstances he confined himself to saying: "Yes, yes, thank you, Mother, I'm getting up now." The wooden door between them must have kept the change in his voice from being noticeable outside, for his mother contented herself with this statement and shuffled away. Yet this brief exchange of words had made the other members of the family aware that Gregor was still in the house, as they had not expected, and at one of the side doors his father was already knocking, gently, yet with his fist. "Gregor, Gregor," he called, "what's the matter with you?" And after a little while he called again in a deeper voice: "Gregor! Gregor!" At the other side door his sister was saying in a low, plaintive tone: "Gregor? Aren't you well? Are you needing anything?" He answered them both at once: "I'm just ready," and did his best to make his voice sound as normal as possible by enunciating the words very clearly and leaving long pauses between them. So his father went back to his breakfast, but his sister whispered: "Gregor, open the door, do." However, he was not thinking of

her übernommene Vorsicht, auch zu Hause alle Türen
während der Nacht zu versperren.

Zunächst wollte er ruhig und ungestört aufstehen, sich
anziehen und vor allem frühstücken, und dann erst das
Weitere überlegen, denn, das merkte er wohl, im Bett
würde er mit dem Nachdenken zu keinem vernünftigen
Ende kommen. Er erinnerte sich, schon öfters im Bett
irgendeinen vielleicht durch ungeschicktes Liegen erzeug-
ten, leichten Schmerz empfunden zu haben, der sich dann
beim Aufstehen als reine Einbildung herausstellte, und er
war gespannt, wie sich seine heutigen Vorstellungen allmählich auflösen würden. Dass die Veränderung der Stimme nichts anderes war als der Vorbote einer tüchtigen
Verkühlung, einer Berufskrankheit der Reisenden, daran
zweifelte er nicht im geringsten.

Die Decke abzuwerfen war ganz einfach; er brauchte
sich nur ein wenig aufzublasen und sie fiel von selbst. Aber
weiterhin wurde es schwierig, besonders weil er so unge-
mein breit war. Er hätte Arme und Hände gebraucht, um
sich aufzurichten; statt dessen aber hatte er nur die vielen
Beinchen, die ununterbrochen in der verschiedensten Bewegung waren und die er überdies nicht beherrschen
konnte. Wollte er eines einmal einknicken, so war es das
erste, dass es sich streckte; und gelang es ihm endlich,
mit diesem Bein das auszuführen, was er wollte, so arbeiteten inzwischen alle anderen, wie freigelassen, in höchster,
schmerzlicher Aufregung. "Nur sich nicht im Bett unnütz
aufhalten", sagte sich Gregor.

Zuerst wollte er mit dem unteren Teil seines Körpers aus
dem Bett hinauskommen, aber dieser untere Teil, den er
übrigens noch nicht gesehen hatte und von dem er sich
auch keine rechte Vorstellung machen konnte, erwies sich
als zu schwer beweglich; es ging so langsam; und als er
schliesslich, fast wild geworden, mit gesammelter Kraft,
ohne Rücksicht sich vorwärtsstiess, hatte er die Richtung
falsch gewählt, schlug an den unteren Bettpfosten heftig

opening the door, and felt thankful for the prudent habit he had acquired in traveling of locking all doors during the night, even at home.

His immediate intention was to get up quietly without being disturbed, to put on his clothes and above all eat his breakfast, and only then to consider what else was to be done, since in bed, he was well aware, his meditations would come to no sensible conclusion. He remembered that often enough in bed he had felt small aches and pains, probably caused by awkward postures, which had proved purely imaginary once he got up, and he looked forward eagerly to seeing this morning's delusions gradually fall away. That the change in his voice was nothing but the precursor of a severe chill, a standing ailment of commercial travelers, he had not the least possible doubt.

To get rid of the quilt was quite easy; he had only to inflate himself a little and it fell off by itself. But the next move was difficult, especially because he was so uncommonly broad. He would have needed arms and hands to hoist himself up; instead he had only the numerous little legs which never stopped waving in all directions and which he could not control in the least. When he tried to bend one of them it was the first to stretch itself straight; and did he succeed at last in making it do what he wanted, all the other legs meanwhile waved the more wildly in a high degree of unpleasant agitation. "But what's the use of lying idle in bed," said Gregor to himself.

He thought that he might get out of bed with the lower part of his body first, but this lower part, which he had not yet seen and of which he could form no clear conception, proved too difficult to move; it shifted so slowly; and when finally, almost wild with annoyance, he gathered his forces together and thrust out recklessly, he had miscalculated the direction and bumped heavily against the lower end of the bed, and the stinging pain

an, und der brennende Schmerz, den er empfand, belehrte ihn, dass gerade der untere Teil seines Körpers augenblicklich vielleicht der empfindlichste war.

Er versuchte es daher, zuerst den Oberkörper aus dem Bett zu bekommen, und drehte vorsichtig den Kopf dem Bettrand zu. Dies gelang auch leicht, und trotz ihrer Breite und Schwere folgte schliesslich die Körpermasse langsam der Wendung des Kopfes. Aber als er den Kopf endlich ausserhalb des Bettes in der freien Luft hielt, bekam er Angst, weiter auf diese Weise vorzurücken, denn wenn er sich schliesslich so fallen liess, musste geradezu ein Wunder geschehen, wenn der Kopf nicht verletzt werden sollte. Und die Besinnung durfte er gerade jetzt um keinen Preis verlieren; lieber wollte er im Bett bleiben.

Aber als er wieder nach gleicher Mühe aufseufzend so dalag wie früher, und wieder seine Beinchen womöglich noch ärger gegeneinander kämpfen sah und keine Möglichkeit fand, in diese Willkür Ruhe und Ordnung zu bringen, sagte er sich wieder, dass er unmöglich im Bett bleiben könne und dass es das Vernünftigste sei, alles zu opfern, wenn auch nur die kleinste Hoffnung bestünde, sich dadurch vom Bett zu befreien. Gleichzeitig aber vergass er nicht, sich zwischendurch daran zu erinnern, dass viel besser als verzweifelte Entschlüsse ruhige und ruhigste Überlegung sei. In solchen Augenblicken richtete er die Augen möglichst scharf auf das Fenster, aber leider war aus dem Anblick des Morgennebels, der sogar die andere Seite der engen Strasse verhüllte, wenig Zuversicht und Munterkeit zu holen. "Schon sieben Uhr," sagte er sich beim neuerlichen Schlagen des Weckers, "schon sieben Uhr und noch immer ein solcher Nebel." Und ein Weilchen lang lag er ruhig mit schwachem Atem, als erwarte er vielleicht von der völligen Stille die Wiederkehr der wirklichen und selbstverständlichen Verhältnisse.

Dann aber sagte er sich: "Ehe es einviertel acht schlägt, muss ich unbedingt das Bett vollständig verlassen haben. Im übrigen wird auch bis dahin jemand aus dem Geschäft

he felt informed him that precisely this lower part of his body was at the moment probably the most sensitive.

So he tried to get the top part of himself out first, and cautiously moved his head towards the edge of the bed. That proved easy enough, and despite its breadth and mass the bulk of his body at last slowly followed the movement of his head. Still, when he finally got his head free over the edge of the bed he felt too scared to go on advancing, for after all if he let himself fall in this way it would take a miracle to keep his head from being injured. And at all costs he must not lose consciousness now, precisely now; he would rather stay in bed.

But when after a repetition of the same efforts he lay in his former position again, sighing, and watched his little legs struggling against each other more wildly than ever, if that were possible, and saw no way of bringing any order into this arbitrary confusion, he told himself again that it was impossible to stay in bed and that the most sensible course was to risk everything for the smallest hope of getting away from it. At the same time he did not forget meanwhile to remind himself that cool reflection, the coolest possible, was much better than desperate resolves. In such moments he focused his eyes as sharply as possible on the window, but, unfortunately, the prospect of the morning fog, which muffled even the other side of the narrow street, brought him little encouragement and comfort. "Seven o'clock already," he said to himself when the alarm clock chimed again, "seven o'clock already and still such a thick fog." And for a little while he lay quiet, breathing lightly, as if perhaps expecting such complete repose to restore all things to their real and normal condition.

But then he said to himself: "Before it strikes a quarter past seven I must be quite out of this bed, without fail. Anyhow, by that time someone will have come from the

kommen, um nach mir zu fragen, denn das Geschäft wird vor sieben Uhr geöffnet." Und er machte sich nun daran, den Körper in seiner ganzen Länge vollständig gleichmässig aus dem Bett hinauszuschaukeln. Wenn er sich auf diese Weise aus dem Bett fallen liess, blieb der Kopf, den er beim Fall scharf heben wollte, voraussichtlich unverletzt. Der Rücken schien hart zu sein; dem würde wohl bei dem Fall auf den Teppich nichts geschehen. Das grösste Bedenken machte ihm die Rücksicht auf den lauten Krach, den es geben müsste und der wahrscheinlich hinter allen Türen wenn nicht Schrecken, so doch Besorgnisse erregen würde. Das musste aber gewagt werden.

Als Gregor schon zur Hälfte aus dem Bette ragte — die neue Methode war mehr ein Spiel als eine Anstrengung, er brauchte immer nur ruckweise zu schaukeln —, fiel ihm ein, wie einfach alles wäre, wenn man ihm zu Hilfe käme. Zwei starke Leute — er dachte an seinen Vater und das Dienstmädchen — hätten vollständig genügt; sie hätten ihre Arme nur unter seinen gewölbten Rücken schieben, ihn so aus dem Bett schälen, sich mit der Last niederbeugen and dann bloss vorsichtig dulden müssen, dass er den Überschwung auf dem Fussboden vollzog, wo dann die Beinchen hoffentlich einen Sinn bekommen würden. Nun, ganz abgesehen davon, dass die Türen versperrt waren, hätte er wirklich um Hilfe rufen sollen? Trotz aller Not konnte er bei diesem Gedanken ein Lächeln nicht unterdrücken.

Schon war er so weit, dass er bei stärkerem Schaukeln kaum das Gleichgewicht noch erhielt, und sehr bald musste er sich nun endgültig entscheiden, denn es war in fünf Minuten einviertel acht, — als es an der Wohnungstür läutete. "Das ist jemand aus dem Geschäft," sagte er sich und erstarrte fast, während seine Beinchen nur desto eiliger tanzten. Einen Augenblick blieb alles still. "Sie öffnen nicht", sagte sich Gregor, befangen in irgendeiner unsinnigen Hoffnung. Aber dann ging natürlich wie immer das Dienstmädchen festen Schrittes zur Tür and öffnete. Gregor brauchte nur das erste Grusswort des Besuchers zu hören

office to ask for me, since it opens before seven." And he set himself to rocking his whole body at once in a regular rhythm, with the idea of swinging it out of the bed. If he tipped himself out in that way he could keep his head from injury by lifting it at an acute angle when he fell. His back seemed to be hard and was not likely to suffer from a fall on the carpet. His biggest worry was the loud crash he would not be able to help making, which would probably cause anxiety, if not terror, behind all the doors. Still, he must take the risk.

When he was already half out of the bed—the new method was more a game than an effort, for he needed only to hitch himself across by rocking to and fro—it struck him how simple it would be if he could get help. Two strong people—he thought of his father and the servant girl—would be amply sufficient; they would only have to thrust their arms under his convex back, lever him out of the bed, bend down with their burden and then be patient enough to let him turn himself right over on to the floor, where it was to be hoped his legs would then find their proper function. Well, ignoring the fact that the doors were all locked, ought he really to call for help? In spite of his misery he could not suppress a smile at the very idea of it.

He had got so far that he could barely keep his equilibrium when he rocked himself strongly, and he would have to nerve himself very soon for the final decision since in five minutes' time it would be a quarter past seven—when the front door bell rang. "That's someone from the office," he said to himself, and grew almost rigid, while his little legs only jigged about all the faster. For a moment everything stayed quiet. "They're not going to open the door," said Gregor to himself, catching at some kind of irrational hope. But then of course the servant girl went as usual to the door with her heavy

und wusste schon, wer es war — der Prokurist selbst. Warum war nur Gregor dazu verurteilt, bei einer Firma zu dienen, wo man bei der kleinsten Versäumnis gleich den grössten Verdacht fasste? Waren denn alle Angestellten samt und sonders Lumpen, gab es denn unter ihnen keinen treuen ergebenen Menschen, der, wenn er auch nur ein paar Morgenstunden für das Geschäft nicht ausgenützt hatte, vor Gewissensbissen närrisch wurde und geradezu nicht imstande war, das Bett zu verlassen? Genügte es wirklich nicht, einen Lehrjungen nachfragen zu lassen — wenn überhaupt diese Fragerei nötig war —, musste da der Prokurist selbst kommen, und musste dadurch der ganzen unschuldigen Familie gezeigt werden, dass die Untersuchung dieser verdächtigen Angelegenheit nur dem Verstand des Prokuristen anvertraut werden konnte? Und mehr infolge der Erregung, in welche Gregor durch diese Überlegungen versetzt wurde, als infolge eines richtigen Entschlusses, schwang er sich mit aller Macht aus dem Bett. Es gab einen lauten Schlag, aber ein eigentlicher Krach war es nicht. Ein wenig wurde der Fall durch den Teppich abgeschwächt, auch war der Rücken elastischer, als Gregor gedacht hatte, daher kam der nicht gar so auffallende dumpfe Klang. Nur den Kopf hatte er nicht vorsichtig genug gehalten und ihn angeschlagen; er drehte ihn und rieb ihn an dem Teppich vor Ärger und Schmerz.

"Da drin ist etwas gefallen", sagte der Prokurist im Nebenzimmer links. Gregor suchte sich vorzustellen, ob nicht auch einmal dem Prokuristen etwas Ähnliches passieren könnte, wie heute ihm; die Möglichkeit dessen musste man doch eigentlich zugeben. Aber wie zur rohen Antwort auf diese Frage machte jetzt der Prokurist im Nebenzimmer ein paar bestimmte Schritte und liess seine Lackstiefel knarren. Aus dem Nebenzimmer rechts flüsterte die Schwester, um Gregor zu verständigen: "Gregor, der Prokurist ist da." "Ich weiss", sagte Gregor vor sich hin; aber so laut, dass es die Schwester hätte hören können, wagte er die Stimme nicht zu erheben.

tread and opened it. Gregor needed only to hear the first good morning of the visitor to know immediately who it was—the chief clerk himself. What a fate, to be condemned to work for a firm where the smallest omission at once gave rise to the gravest suspicion! Were all employees in a body nothing but scoundrels, was there not among them one single loyal devoted man who, had he wasted only an hour or so of the firm's time in a morning, was so tormented by conscience as to be driven out of his mind and actually incapable of leaving his bed? Wouldn't it really have been sufficient to send an apprentice to inquire—if any inquiry were necessary at all—did the chief clerk himself have to come and thus indicate to the entire family, an innocent family, that this suspicious circumstance could be investigated by no one less versed in affairs than himself? And more through the agitation caused by these reflections than through any act of will Gregor swung himself out of bed with all his strength. There was a loud thump, but it was not really a crash. His fall was broken to some extent by the carpet, his back, too, was less stiff than he thought, and so there was merely a dull thud, not so very startling. Only he had not lifted his head carefully enough and had hit it; he turned it and rubbed it on the carpet in pain and irritation.

"That was something falling down in there," said the chief clerk in the next room to the left. Gregor tried to suppose to himself that something like what had happened to him today might some day happen to the chief clerk; one really could not deny that it was possible. But as if in brusque reply to this supposition the chief clerk took a couple of firm steps in the next-door room and his patent leather boots creaked. From the right-hand room his sister was whispering to inform him of the situation: "Gregor, the chief clerk's here." "I know," muttered Gregor to himself; but he didn't dare to make his voice loud enough for his sister to hear it.

"Gregor," sagte nun der Vater aus dem Nebenzimmer links, "der Herr Prokurist ist gekommen und erkundigt sich, warum du nicht mit dem Frühzug weggefahren bist. Wir wissen nicht, was wir ihm sagen sollen. Übrigens will er auch mit dir persönlich sprechen. Also bitte mach die Tür auf. Er wird die Unordnung im Zimmer zu entschuldigen schon die Güte haben." "Guten Morgen, Herr Samsa", rief der Prokurist freundlich dazwischen. "Ihm ist nicht wohl," sagte die Mutter zum Prokuristen, während der Vater noch an der Tür redete, "ihm ist nicht wohl, glauben Sie mir, Herr Prokurist. Wie würde denn Gregor sonst einen Zug versäumen! Der Junge hat ja nichts im Kopf als das Geschäft. Ich ärgere mich schon fast, dass er abends niemals ausgeht; jetzt war er doch acht Tage in der Stadt, aber jeden Abend war er zu Hause. Da sitzt er bei uns am Tisch und liest still die Zeitung oder studiert Fahrpläne. Es ist schon eine Zerstreuung für ihn, wenn er sich mit Laubsägearbeiten beschäftigt. Da hat er zum Beispiel im Laufe von zwei, drei Abenden einen kleinen Rahmen geschnitzt; Sie werden staunen, wie hübsch er ist; er hängt drin im Zimmer; Sie werden ihn gleich sehen, bis Gregor aufmacht. Ich bin übrigens glücklich, dass Sie da sind, Herr Prokurist; wir allein hätten Gregor nicht dazu gebracht, die Tür zu öffnen; er ist so hartnäckig; und bestimmt ist ihm nicht wohl, trotzdem er es am Morgen geleugnet hat." "Ich komme gleich", sagte Gregor langsam und bedächtig und rührte sich nicht, um kein Wort der Gespräche zu verlieren. "Anders, gnädige Frau, kann ich es mir auch nicht erklären," sagte der Prokurist, "hoffentlich ist es nichts Ernstes. Wenn ich auch andererseits sagen muss, dass wir Geschäftsleute — wie man will, leider oder glücklicherweise — ein leichtes Unwohlsein sehr oft aus geschäftlichen Rücksichten einfach überwinden müssen." "Also kann der Herr Prokurist schon zu dir hinein?" fragte der ungeduldige Vater und klopfte wiederum an die Tür. "Nein", sagte Gregor. Im Nebenzimmer links trat eine peinliche Stille ein, im Nebenzimmer rechts begann die Schwester zu schluchzen.

"Gregor," said his father now from the left-hand room, "the chief clerk has come and wants to know why you didn't catch the early train. We don't know what to say to him. Besides, he wants to talk to you in person. So open the door, please. He will be good enough to excuse the untidiness of your room." "Good morning, Mr. Samsa," the chief clerk was calling amiably meanwhile. "He's not well," said his mother to the visitor, while his father was still speaking through the door, "he's not well, sir, believe me. What else would make him miss a train! The boy thinks about nothing but his work. It makes me almost cross the way he never goes out in the evenings; he's been here the last eight days and has stayed at home every single evening. He just sits there quietly at the table reading a newspaper or looking through railway timetables. The only amusement he gets is doing fretwork. For instance, he spent two or three evenings cutting out a little picture frame; you would be surprised to see how pretty it is; it's hanging in his room; you'll see it in a minute when Gregor opens the door. I must say I'm glad you've come, sir; we should never have got him to unlock the door by ourselves; he's so obstinate; and I'm sure he's unwell, though he wouldn't have it to be so this morning." "I'm just coming," said Gregor slowly and carefully, not moving an inch for fear of losing one word of the conversation. "I can't think of any other explanation, madam," said the chief clerk, "I hope it's nothing serious. Although on the other hand I must say that we men of business—fortunately or unfortunately—very often simply have to ignore any slight indisposition, since business must be attended to." "Well, can the chief clerk come in now?" asked Gregor's father impatiently, again knocking on the door. "No," said Gregor. In the left-hand room a painful silence followed this refusal, in the right-hand room his sister began to sob.

Warum ging denn die Schwester nicht zu den anderen?
Sie war wohl erst jetzt aus dem Bett aufgestanden und
hatte noch gar nicht angefangen sich anzuziehen. Und
warum weinte sie denn? Weil er nicht aufstand und den
Prokuristen nicht hereinliess, weil er in Gefahr war, den
Posten zu verlieren und weil dann der Chef die Eltern
mit den alten Forderungen wieder verfolgen würde? Das
waren doch vorläufig wohl unnötige Sorgen. Noch war
Gregor hier und dachte nicht im geringsten daran, seine
Familie zu verlassen. Augenblicklich lag er wohl da auf
dem Teppich, und niemand, der seinen Zustand gekannt
hätte, hätte im Ernst von ihm verlangt, dass er den Prokuristen hereinlasse. Aber wegen dieser kleinen Unhöflichkeit,
für die sich ja später leicht eine passende Ausrede finden
würde, konnte Gregor doch nicht gut sofort weggeschickt
werden. Und Gregor schien es, dass es viel vernünftiger
wäre, ihn jetzt in Ruhe zu lassen, statt ihn mit Weinen
und Zureden zu stören. Aber es war eben die Ungewissheit,
welche die anderen bedrängte and ihr Benehmen ent-
schuldigte.

"Herr Samsa," rief nun der Prokurist mit erhobener
Stimme, "was ist denn los? Sie verbarrikadieren sich da in
Ihrem Zimmer, antworten bloss mit ja und nein, machen
Ihren Eltern schwere, unnötige Sorgen und versäumen —
dies nur nebenbei erwähnt — Ihre geschäftlichen Pflichten
in einer eigentlich unerhörten Weise. Ich spreche hier im
Namen Ihrer Eltern und Ihres Chefs und bitte Sie ganz
ernsthaft um eine augenblickliche, deutliche Erklärung.
Ich staune, ich staune. Ich glaubte Sie als einen ruhigen,
vernünftigen Menschen zu kennen, und nun scheinen Sie
plötzlich anfangen zu wollen, mit sonderbaren Launen zu
paradieren. Der Chef deutete mir zwar heute früh eine
mögliche Erklärung für Ihre Versäumnis an — sie betraf
das Ihnen seit kurzem anvertraute Inkasso —, aber ich
legte wahrhaftig fast mein Ehrenwort dafür ein, dass diese
Erklärung nicht zutreffen könne. Nun aber sehe ich hier
Ihren unbegreiflichen Starrsinn und verliere ganz und gar

Why didn't his sister join the others? She was probably newly out of bed and hadn't even begun to put on
her clothes yet. Well, why was she crying? Because he
wouldn't get up and let the chief clerk in, because he
was in danger of losing his job, and because the chief
would begin dunning his parents again for the old
debts? Surely these were things one didn't need to worry
about for the present. Gregor was still at home and not
in the least thinking of deserting the family. At the moment, true, he was lying on the carpet and no one who
knew the condition he was in could seriously expect him
to admit the chief clerk. But for such a small discourtesy,
which could plausibly be explained away somehow later
on, Gregor could hardly be dismissed on the spot. And it
seemed to Gregor that it would be much more sensible
to leave him in peace for the present than to trouble
him with tears and entreaties. Still, of course, their un-
certainty bewildered them all and excused their behavior.

"Mr. Samsa," the chief clerk called now in a louder
voice, "what's the matter with you? Here you are, bar-
ricading yourself in your room, giving only 'yes' and
'no' for answers, causing your parents a lot of unnecessary trouble and neglecting—I mention this only in pass-
ing—neglecting your business duties in an incredible
fashion. I am speaking here in the name of your parents
and of your chief, and I beg you quite seriously to give
me an immediate and precise explanation. You amaze me,
you amaze me. I thought you were a quiet, dependable
person, and now all at once you seem bent on making a
disgraceful exhibition of yourself. The chief did hint to
me early this morning a possible explanation for your
disappearance—with reference to the cash payments that
were entrusted to you recently—but I almost pledged
my solemn word of honor that this could not be so.
But now that I see how incredibly obstinate you are, I

jede Lust, mich auch nur im geringsten für Sie einzusetzen. Und Ihre Stellung ist durchaus nicht die festeste. Ich hatte ursprünglich die Absicht, Ihnen das alles unter vier Augen zu sagen, aber da Sie mich hier nutzlos meine Zeit versäumen lassen, weiss ich nicht, warum es nicht auch Ihre Herren Eltern erfahren sollen. Ihre Leistungen in der letzten Zeit waren also sehr unbefriedigend; es ist zwar nicht die Jahreszeit, um besondere Geschäfte zu machen, das erkennen wir an; aber eine Jahreszeit, um keine Geschäfte zu machen, gibt es überhaupt nicht, Herr Samsa, darf es nicht geben."

"Aber Herr Prokurist," rief Gregor ausser sich und vergass in der Aufregung alles andere, "ich mache ja sofort, augenblicklich auf. Ein leichtes Unwohlsein, ein Schwindelanfall, haben mich verhindert aufzustehen. Ich liege noch jetzt im Bett. Jetzt bin ich aber schon wieder ganz frisch. Eben steige ich aus dem Bett. Nur einen kleinen Augenblick Geduld! Es geht noch nicht so gut, wie ich dachte. Es ist mir aber schon wohl. Wie das nur einen Menschen so überfallen kann! Noch gestern abend war mir ganz gut, meine Eltern wissen es ja, oder besser, schon gestern abend hatte ich eine kleine Vorahnung. Man hätte es mir ansehen müssen. Warum habe ich es nur im Geschäft nicht gemeldet! Aber man denkt eben immer, dass man die Krankheit ohne Zuhausebleiben überstehen wird. Herr Prokurist! Schonen Sie meine Eltern! Für alle die Vorwürfe, die Sie mir jetzt machen, ist ja kein Grund; man hat mir ja davon auch kein Wort gesagt. Sie haben vielleicht die letzten Aufträge, die ich geschickt habe, nicht gelesen. Übrigens, noch mit dem Achtuhrzug fahre ich auf die Reise, die paar Stunden Ruhe haben mich gekräftigt. Halten Sie sich nur nicht auf, Herr Prokurist; ich bin gleich selbst im Geschäft, und haben Sie die Güte, das zu sagen und mich dem Herrn Chef zu empfehlen!"

Und während Gregor dies alles hastig ausstiess und kaum wusste, was er sprach, hatte er sich leicht, wohl infolge der im Bett bereits erlangten Übung, dem Kasten genähert und

no longer have the slightest desire to take your part at all. And your position in the firm is not so unassailable. I came with the intention of telling you all this in private, but since you are wasting my time so needlessly I don't see why your parents shouldn't hear it too. For some time past your work has been most unsatisfactory; this is not the season of the year for a business boom, of course, we admit that, but a season of the year for doing no business at all, that does not exist, Mr. Samsa, must not exist."

"But, sir," cried Gregor, beside himself and in his agitation forgetting everything else, "I'm just going to open the door this very minute. A slight illness, an attack of giddiness, has kept me from getting up. I'm still lying in bed. But I feel all right again. I'm getting out of bed now. Just give me a moment or two longer! I'm not quite so well as I thought. But I'm all right, really. How a thing like that can suddenly strike one down! Only last night I was quite well, my parents can tell you, or rather I did have a slight presentiment. I must have showed some sign of it. Why didn't I report it at the office! But one always thinks that an indisposition can be got over without staying in the house. Oh sir, do spare my parents! All that you're reproaching me with now has no foundation; no one has ever said a word to me about it. Perhaps you haven't looked at the last orders I sent in. Anyhow, I can still catch the eight o'clock train, I'm much the better for my few hours' rest. Don't let me detain you here, sir; I'll be attending to business very soon, and do be good enough to tell the chief so and to make my excuses to him!"

And while all this was tumbling out pell-mell and Gregor hardly knew what he was saying, he had reached the chest quite easily, perhaps because of the practice

versuchte nun, an ihm sich aufzurichten. Er wollte tatsächlich die Tür aufmachen, tatsächlich sich sehen lassen und
mit dem Prokuristen sprechen; er war begierig zu erfahren,
was die anderen, die jetzt so nach ihm verlangten, bei seinem
Anblick sagen würden. Würden sie erschrecken, dann hatte
Gregor keine Verantwortung mehr und konnte ruhig sein.
Würden sie aber alles ruhig hinnehmen, dann hatte auch
er keinen Grund sich aufzuregen, und konnte, wenn er
sich beeilte, um acht Uhr tatsächlich auf dem Bahnhof sein.
Zuerst glitt er nun einigemale von dem glatten Kasten ab,
aber endlich gab er sich einen letzten Schwung und stand
aufrecht da; auf die Schmerzen im Unterleib achtete er
gar nicht mehr, so sehr sie auch brannten. Nun liess er sich
gegen die Rückenlehne eines nahen Stuhles fallen, an deren
Rändern er sich mit seinen Beinchen festhielt. Damit hatte
er aber auch die Herrschaft über sich erlangt und verstummte, denn nun konnte er den Prokuristen anhören.

"Haben Sie auch nur ein Wort verstanden?" fragte der
Prokurist die Eltern, "er macht sich doch wohl nicht einen
Narren aus uns?" "Um Gottes willen," rief die Mutter
schon unter Weinen, "er ist vielleicht schwer krank, und
wir quälen ihn. Grete! Grete!" schrie sie dann. "Mutter?"
rief die Schwester von der anderen Seite. Sie verständigten
sich durch Gregors Zimmer. "Du musst augenblicklich zum
Arzt. Gregor ist krank. Rasch um den Arzt. Hast du
Gregor jetzt reden hören?" "Das war eine Tierstimme",
sagte der Prokurist, auffallend leise gegenüber dem Schreien
der Mutter. "Anna! Anna!" rief der Vater durch das Vorzimmer in die Küche und klatschte in die Hände, "sofort
einen Schlosser holen!" Und schon liefen die zwei Mädchen
mit rauschenden Röcken durch das Vorzimmer — wie
hatte sich die Schwester denn so schnell angezogen? —
und rissen die Wohnungstür auf. Man hörte gar nicht die
Türe zuschlagen; sie hatten sie wohl offen gelassen, wie es
in Wohnungen zu sein pflegt, in denen ein grosses Unglück
geschehen ist.

he had had in bed, and was now trying to lever himself upright by means of it. He meant actually to open the door, actually to show himself and speak to the chief clerk; he was eager to find out what the others, after all their insistence, would say at the sight of him. If they were horrified then the responsibility was no longer his and he could stay quiet. But if they took it calmly, then he had no reason either to be upset, and could really get to the station for the eight o'clock train if he hurried. At first he slipped down a few times from the polished surface of the chest, but at length with a last heave he stood upright; he paid no more attention to the pains in the lower part of his body, however they smarted. Then he let himself fall against the back of a near-by chair, and clung with his little legs to the edges of it. That brought him into control of himself again and he stopped speaking, for now he could listen to what the chief clerk was saying.

"Did you understand a word of it?" the chief clerk was asking; "surely he can't be trying to make fools of us?" "Oh dear," cried his mother, in tears, "perhaps he's terribly ill and we're tormenting him. Grete! Grete!" she called out then. "Yes Mother?" called his sister from the other side. They were calling to each other across Gregor's room. "You must go this minute for the doctor. Gregor is ill. Go for the doctor, quick. Did you hear how he was speaking?" "That was no human voice," said the chief clerk in a voice noticeably low beside the shrillness of the mother's. "Anna! Anna!" his father was calling through the hall to the kitchen, clapping his hands, "get a locksmith at once!" And the two girls were already running through the hall with a swish of skirts—how could his sister have got dressed so quickly? —and were tearing the front door open. There was no sound of its closing again; they had evidently left it open, as one does in houses where some great misfortune has happened.

Gregor war aber viel ruhiger geworden. Man verstand
zwar also seine Worte nicht mehr, trotzdem sie ihm genug
klar, klarer als früher, vorgekommen waren, vielleicht infolge der Gewöhnung des Ohres. Aber immerhin glaubte
man nun schon daran, dass es mit ihm nicht ganz in Ordnung war, und war bereit, ihm zu helfen. Die Zuversicht
und Sicherheit, mit welchen die ersten Anordnungen ge-
troffen worden waren, taten ihm wohl. Er fühlte sich wieder
einbezogen in den menschlichen Kreis und erhoffte von
beiden, vom Arzt und vom Schlosser, ohne sie eigentlich
genau zu scheiden, grossartige und überraschende Leistungen. Um für die sich nähernden entscheidenden Be-
sprechungen eine möglichst klare Stimme zu bekommen,
hustete er ein wenig ab, allerdings bemüht, dies ganz ge-
dämpft zu tun, da möglicherweise auch schon dieses Geräusch anders als menschlicher Husten klang, was er selbst
zu entscheiden sich nicht mehr getraute. Im Nebenzimmer
war es inzwischen ganz still geworden. Vielleicht sassen
die Eltern mit dem Prokuristen beim Tisch und tuschelten,
vielleicht lehnten alle an der Türe und horchten.

Gregor schob sich langsam mit dem Sessel zur Tür hin,
liess ihn dort los, warf sich gegen die Tür, hielt sich an
ihr aufrecht — die Ballen seiner Beinchen hatten ein wenig
Klebstoff — und ruhte sich dort einen Augenblick lang
von der Anstrengung aus. Dann aber machte er sich daran,
mit dem Mund den Schlüssel im Schloss umzudrehen. Es
schien leider, dass er keine eigentlichen Zähne hatte, —
womit sollte er gleich den Schlüssel fassen? — aber dafür
waren die Kiefer freilich sehr stark; mit ihrer Hilfe brachte
er auch wirklich den Schlüssel in Bewegung und achtete
nicht darauf, dass er sich zweifellos irgendeinen Schaden
zufügte, denn eine braune Flüssigkeit kam ihm aus dem
Mund, floss über den Schlüssel und tropfte auf den Boden.
"Hören Sie nur," sagte der Prokurist im Nebenzimmer, "er
dreht den Schlüssel um." Das war für Gregor eine grosse
Aufmunterung; aber alle hätten ihm zurufen sollen, auch
der Vater und die Mutter: "Frisch, Gregor," hätten sie

But Gregor was now much calmer. The words he uttered were no longer understandable, apparently, although they seemed clear enough to him, even clearer than before, perhaps because his ear had grown accustomed to the sound of them. Yet at any rate people now believed that something was wrong with him, and were ready to help him. The positive certainty with which these first measures had been taken comforted him. He felt himself drawn once more into the human circle and hoped for great and remarkable results from both the doctor and the locksmith, without really distinguishing precisely between them. To make his voice as clear as possible for the decisive conversation that was now imminent he coughed a little, as quietly as he could, of course, since this noise too might not sound like a human cough for all he was able to judge. In the next room meanwhile there was complete silence. Perhaps his parents were sitting at the table with the chief clerk, whispering, perhaps they were all leaning against the door and listening.

Slowly Gregor pushed the chair towards the door, then let go of it, caught hold of the door for support—the soles at the end of his little legs were somewhat sticky—and rested against it for a moment after his efforts. Then he set himself to turning the key in the lock with his mouth. It seemed, unhappily, that he hadn't really any teeth—what could he grip the key with?—but on the other hand his jaws were certainly very strong; with their help he did manage to set the key in motion, heedless of the fact that he was undoubtedly damaging them somehow, since a brown fluid issued from his mouth, flowed over the key and dripped on the floor. "Just listen to that," said the chief clerk next door; "he's turning the key." That was a great encouragement to Gregor; but they should all have shouted encouragement to him, his father and mother too: "Go on, Gregor," they should have called out, "keep going,

rufen sollen, "immer nur heran, fest an das Schloss heran!"
Und in der Vorstellung, dass alle seine Bemühungen mit
Spannung verfolgten, verbiss er sich mit allem, was er an
Kraft aufbringen konnte, besinnungslos in den Schlüssel.
Je nach dem Fortschreiten der Drehung des Schlüssels um-
tanzte er das Schloss; hielt sich jetzt nur noch mit dem
Munde aufrecht, und je nach Bedarf hing er sich an
den Schlüssel oder drückte ihn dann wieder nieder mit der
ganzen Last seines Körpers. Der hellere Klang des endlich
zurückschnappenden Schlosses erweckte Gregor förmlich.
Aufatmend sagte er sich: "Ich habe also den Schlosser nicht
gebraucht", und legte den Kopf auf die Klinke, um die
Türe gänzlich zu öffnen.

Da er die Türe auf diese Weise öffnen musste, war sie
eigentlich schon recht weit geöffnet, und er selbst noch
nicht zu sehen. Er musste sich erst langsam um den einen
Türflügel herumdrehen, und zwar sehr vorsichtig, wenn er
nicht gerade vor dem Eintritt ins Zimmer plump auf den
Rücken fallen wollte. Er war noch mit jener schwierigen
Bewegung beschäftigt und hatte nicht Zeit, auf anderes zu
achten, da hörte er schon den Prokuristen ein lautes "Oh!"
ausstossen — es klang, wie wenn der Wind saust — und
nun sah er ihn auch, wie er, der der Nächste an der Türe
war, die Hand gegen den offenen Mund drückte und langsam zurückwich, als vertreibe ihn eine unsichtbare, gleichmässig fortwirkende Kraft. Die Mutter — sie stand hier
trotz der Anwesenheit des Prokuristen mit von der Nacht
her noch aufgelösten, hoch sich sträubenden Haaren —
sah zuerst mit gefalteten Händen den Vater an, ging dann
zwei Schritte zu Gregor hin und fiel inmitten ihrer rings
um sie herum sich ausbreitenden Röcke nieder, das Gesicht
ganz unauffindbar zu ihrer Brust gesenkt. Der Vater ballte
mit feindseligem Ausdruck die Faust, als wolle er Gregor in
sein Zimmer zurückstossen, sah sich dann unsicher im
Wohnzimmer um, beschattete dann mit den Händen die
Augen und weinte, dass sich seine mächtige Brust
schüttelte.

hold on to that key!" And in the belief that they were all following his efforts intently, he clenched his jaws recklessly on the key with all the force at his command. As the turning of the key progressed he circled round the lock, holding on now only with his mouth, pushing on the key, as required, or pulling it down again with all the weight of his body. The louder click of the finally yielding lock literally quickened Gregor. With a deep breath of relief he said to himself: "So I didn't need the locksmith," and laid his head on the handle to open the door wide.

Since he had to pull the door towards him, he was still invisible when it was really wide open. He had to edge himself slowly round the near half of the double door, and to do it very carefully if he was not to fall plump upon his back just on the threshold. He was still carrying out this difficult maneuver, with no time to observe anything else, when he heard the chief clerk utter a loud "Oh!"—it sounded like a gust of wind—and now he could see the man, standing as he was nearest to the door, clapping one hand before his open mouth and slowly backing away as if driven by some invisible steady pressure. His mother—in spite of the chief clerk's being there her hair was still undone and sticking up in all directions—first clasped her hands and looked at his father, then took two steps towards Gregor and fell on the floor among her outspread skirts, her face quite hidden on her breast. His father knotted his fist with a fierce expression on his face as if he meant to knock Gregor back into his room, then looked uncertainly round the living room, covered his eyes with his hands and wept till his great chest heaved.

Gregor trat nun gar nicht in das Zimmer, sondern lehnte sich von innen an den festgeriegelten Türflügel, so dass sein Leib nur zur Hälfte und darüber der seitlich geneigte Kopf zu sehen war, mit dem er zu den anderen hinüberlugte. Es war inzwischen viel heller geworden; klar stand auf der anderen Strassenseite ein Ausschnitt des gegenüberliegenden, endlosen, grauschwarzen Hauses — es war ein Krankenhaus — mit seinen hart die Front durchbrechenden regelmässigen Fenstern; der Regen fiel noch nieder, aber nur mit grossen, einzeln sichtbaren und förmlich auch einzelnweise auf die Erde hinuntergeworfenen Tropfen. Das Frühstücksgeschirr stand in überreicher Zahl auf dem Tisch, denn für den Vater war das Frühstück die wichtigste Mahlzeit des Tages, die er bei der Lektüre verschiedener Zeitungen stundenlang hinzog. Gerade an der gegenüberliegenden Wand hing eine Photographie Gregors aus seiner Militärzeit, die ihn als Leutnant darstellte, wie er, die Hand am Degen, sorglos lächelnd, Respekt für seine Haltung und Uniform verlangte. Die Tür zum Vorzimmer war geöffnet, und man sah, da auch die Wohnungstür offen war, auf den Vorplatz der Wohnung hinaus und auf den Beginn der abwärts führenden Treppe.

"Nun," sagte Gregor und war sich dessen wohl bewusst, dass er der einzige war, der die Ruhe bewahrt hatte, "ich werde mich gleich anziehen, die Kollektion zusammenpakken und wegfahren. Wollt ihr, wollt ihr mich wegfahren lassen? Nun, Herr Prokurist, Sie sehen, ich bin nicht starrköpfig und ich arbeite gern; das Reisen ist beschwerlich, aber ich könnte ohne das Reisen nicht leben. Wohin gehen Sie denn, Herr Prokurist? Ins Geschäft? Ja? Werden Sie alles wahrheitsgetreu berichten? Man kann im Augenblick unfähig sein zu arbeiten, aber dann ist gerade der richtige Zeitpunkt, sich an die früheren Leistungen zu erinnern und zu bedenken, dass man später, nach Beseitigung des Hindernisses, gewiss desto fleissiger und gesammelter arbeiten wird. Ich bin ja dem Herrn Chef so sehr verpflichtet, das wissen Sie doch recht gut. Andererseits habe ich die Sorge

Gregor did not go now into the living room, but leaned against the inside of the firmly shut wing of the door, so that only half his body was visible and his head above it bending sideways to look at the others. The light had meanwhile strengthened; on the other side of the street one could see clearly a section of the endlessly long, dark gray building opposite—it was a hospital—abruptly punctuated by its row of regular windows; the rain was still falling, but only in large singly discernible and literally singly splashing drops. The breakfast dishes were set out on the table lavishly, for breakfast was the most important meal of the day to Gregor's father, who lingered it out for hours over various newspapers. Right opposite Gregor on the wall hung a photograph of himself on military service, as a lieutenant, hand on sword, a carefree smile on his face, inviting one to respect his uniform and military bearing. The door leading to the hall was open, and one could see that the front door stood open too, showing the landing beyond and the beginning of the stairs going down.

"Well," said Gregor, knowing perfectly that he was the only one who had retained any composure, "I'll put my clothes on at once, pack up my samples and start off. Will you only let me go? You see, sir, I'm not obstinate, and I'm willing to work; traveling is a hard life, but I couldn't live without it. Where are you going, sir? To the office? Yes? Will you give a true account of all this? One can be temporarily incapacitated, but that's just the moment for remembering former services and bearing in mind that later on, when the incapacity has been got over, one will certainly work with all the more industry and concentration. I'm loyally bound to serve the chief, you know that very well. Besides, I have to provide for my parents and my sister. I'm in great difficulties, but I'll get out of them again. Don't make things

um meine Eltern und die Schwester. Ich bin in der Klemme, ich werde mich aber auch wieder herausarbeiten. Machen Sie es mir aber nicht schwieriger, als es schon ist. Halten Sie im Geschäft meine Partei! Man liebt den Reisenden nicht, ich weiss. Man denkt, er verdient ein Heidengeld und führt dabei ein schönes Leben. Man hat eben keine besondere Veranlassung, dieses Vorurteil besser zu durchdenken. Sie aber, Herr Prokurist, Sie haben einen besseren Überblick über die Verhältnisse, als das übrige Personal, ja sogar, ganz im Vertrauen gesagt, einen besseren Überblick als der Herr Chef selbst, der in seiner Eigenschaft als Unternehmer sich in seinem Urteil leicht zuungunsten eines Angestellten beirren lässt. Sie wissen auch sehr wohl, dass der Reisende, der fast das ganze Jahr ausserhalb des Geschäftes ist, so leicht ein Opfer von Klatschereien, Zufälligkeiten und grundlosen Beschwerden werden kann, gegen die sich zu wehren ihm ganz unmöglich ist, da er von ihnen meistens gar nichts erfährt und nur dann, wenn er erschöpft eine Reise beendet hat, zu Hause die schlimmen, auf ihre Ursachen hin nicht mehr zu durchschauenden Folgen am eigenen Leibe zu spüren bekommt. Herr Prokurist, gehen Sie nicht weg, ohne mir ein Wort gesagt zu haben, das mir zeigt, dass Sie mir wenigstens zu einem kleinen Teil recht geben!"

Aber der Prokurist hatte sich schon bei den ersten Worten Gregors abgewendet, und nur über die zuckende Schulter hinweg sah er mit aufgeworfenen Lippen nach Gregor zurück. Und während Gregors Rede stand er keinen Augenblick still, sondern verzog sich, ohne Gregor aus den Augen zu lassen, gegen die Tür, aber ganz allmählich, als bestehe ein geheimes Verbot, das Zimmer zu verlassen. Schon war er im Vorzimmer, und nach der plötzlichen Bewegung, mit der er zum letztenmal den Fuss aus dem Wohnzimmer zog, hätte man glauben können, er habe sich soeben die Sohle verbrannt. Im Vorzimmer aber streckte er die rechte Hand weit von sich zur Treppe hin, als warte dort auf ihn eine geradezu überirdische Erlösung.

Gregor sah ein, dass er den Prokuristen in dieser Stim-

any worse for me than they are. Stand up for me in the firm. Travelers are not popular, I know. People think they earn sacks of money and just have a good time. And there seems to be no particular reason to revise this prejudice. But you, sir, have a more comprehensive view of affairs than the rest of the staff, yes, let me tell you in confidence, a more comprehensive view than the chief himself, who, being the owner, lets his judgment easily be swayed against one of his employees. And you know very well that the traveler, who is never seen in the office almost the whole year round, can so easily fall a victim to gossip and ill luck and unfounded complaints, which he mostly knows nothing about, except when he comes back exhausted from his rounds, and only then suffers in person from their evil consequences, which he can no longer trace back to the original causes. Sir, sir, don't go away without a word to me to show that you think me in the right at least to some extent!"

But at Gregor's very first words the chief clerk had already backed away and only stared at him with parted lips over one twitching shoulder. And while Gregor was speaking he did not stand still one moment but stole away towards the door, without taking his eyes off Gregor, yet only an inch at a time, as if obeying some secret injunction to leave the room. He was already at the hall, and the suddenness with which he took his last step out of the living room would have made one believe he had burned the sole of his foot. Once in the hall he stretched his right arm before him towards the staircase, as if some supernatural power were waiting there to deliver him.

Gregor perceived that the chief clerk must on no ac-

mung auf keinen Fall weggehen lassen dürfe, wenn dadurch
seine Stellung im Geschäft nicht aufs äusserste gefährdet
werden sollte. Die Eltern verstanden das alles nicht so gut;
sie hatten sich in den langen Jahren die Überzeugung ge-
bildet, dass Gregor in diesem Geschäft für sein Leben
versorgt war, und hatten ausserdem jetzt mit den augen-
blicklichen Sorgen so viel zu tun, dass ihnen jede Voraussicht abhanden gekommen war. Aber Gregor hatte diese
Voraussicht. Der Prokurist musste gehalten, beruhigt,
überzeugt und schliesslich gewonnen werden; die Zukunft
Gregors und seiner Familie hing doch davon ab! Wäre doch
die Schwester hier gewesen! Sie war klug; sie hatte schon
geweint, als Gregor noch ruhig auf dem Rücken lag. Und
gewiss hätte der Prokurist, dieser Damenfreund, sich von
ihr lenken lassen; sie hätte die Wohnungstür zugemacht
und ihm im Vorzimmer den Schrecken ausgeredet. Aber
die Schwester war eben nicht da, Gregor selbst musste han-
deln. Und ohne daran zu denken, dass er seine gegenwärtigen Fähigkeiten, sich zu bewegen, noch gar nicht kannte,
ohne auch daran zu denken, dass seine Rede möglicher- ja
wahrscheinlicherweise wieder nicht verstanden worden war,
verliess er den Türflügel; schob sich durch die Öffnung;
wollte zum Prokuristen hingehen, der sich schon am Geländer des Vorplatzes lächerlicherweise mit beiden Händen
festhielt; fiel aber sofort, nach einem Halt suchend, mit
einem kleinen Schrei auf seine vielen Beinchen nieder.
Kaum war das geschehen, fühlte er zum erstenmal an diesem Morgen ein körperliches Wohlbehagen; die Beinchen
hatten festen Boden unter sich; sie gehorchten vollkommen,
wie er zu seiner Freude merkte; strebten sogar darnach,
ihn fortzutragen, wohin er wollte; und schon glaubte er,
die endgültige Besserung alles Leidens stehe unmittelbar
bevor. Aber im gleichen Augenblick, als er da schaukelnd
vor verhaltener Bewegung, gar nicht weit von seiner Mutter
entfernt, ihr gerade gegenüber auf dem Boden lag, sprang
diese, die doch so ganz in sich versunken schien, mit einem-
male in die Höhe, die Arme weit ausgestreckt, die Finger

count be allowed to go away in this frame of mind if his position in the firm were not to be endangered to the utmost. His parents did not understand this so well; they had convinced themselves in the course of years that Gregor was settled for life in this firm, and besides they were so preoccupied with their immediate troubles that all foresight had forsaken them. Yet Gregor had this foresight. The chief clerk must be detained, soothed, persuaded and finally won over; the whole future of Gregor and his family depended on it! If only his sister had been there! She was intelligent; she had begun to cry while Gregor was still lying quietly on his back. And no doubt the chief clerk, so partial to ladies, would have been guided by her; she would have shut the door of the flat and in the hall talked him out of his horror. But she was not there, and Gregor would have to handle the situation himself. And without remembering that he was still unaware what powers of movement he possessed, without even remembering that his words in all possibility, indeed in all likelihood, would again be unintelligible, he let go the wing of the door, pushed himself through the opening, started to walk towards the chief clerk, who was already ridiculously clinging with both hands to the railing on the landing; but immediately, as he was feeling for a support, he fell down with a little cry upon all his numerous legs. Hardly was he down when he experienced for the first time this morning a sense of physical comfort; his legs had firm ground under them; they were completely obedient, as he noted with joy; they even strove to carry him forward in whatever direction he chose; and he was inclined to believe that a final relief from all his sufferings was at hand. But in the same moment as he found himself on the floor, rocking with suppressed eagerness to move, not far from his mother, indeed just in front of her, she, who had seemed so completely crushed, sprang all at once to her feet, her arms and fingers outspread, cried:

gespreizt, rief "Hilfe, um Gottes willen, Hilfe!", hielt den
Kopf geneigt, als wolle sie Gregor besser sehen, lief aber,
im Widerspruch dazu, sinnlos zurück; hatte vergessen, dass
hinter ihr der gedeckte Tisch stand; setzte sich, als sie bei
ihm angekommen war, wie in Zerstreutheit, eilig auf ihn;
und schien gar nicht zu merken, dass neben ihr aus der
umgeworfenen grossen Kanne der Kaffee in vollem Strome
auf den Teppich sich ergoss.

   "Mutter, Mutter", sagte Gregor leise und sah zu ihr hinauf. Der Prokurist war ihm für einen Augenblick ganz aus
dem Sinn gekommen; dagegen konnte er sich nicht ver-
sagen, im Anblick des fliessenden Kaffees mehrmals mit
den Kiefern ins Leere zu schnappen. Darüber schrie die
Mutter neuerdings auf, flüchtete vom Tisch und fiel dem
ihr entgegeneilenden Vater in die Arme. Aber Gregor hatte
jetzt keine Zeit für seine Eltern; der Prokurist war schon
auf der Treppe; das Kinn auf dem Geländer, sah er noch
zum letzten Male zurück. Gregor nahm einen Anlauf, um
ihn möglichst sicher einzuholen; der Prokurist musste etwas
ahnen, denn er machte einen Sprung über mehrere Stufen
und verschwand; "Huh!" aber schrie er noch, es klang
durchs ganze Treppenhaus. Leider schien nun auch diese
Flucht des Prokuristen den Vater, der bisher verhältnismässig gefasst gewesen war, völlig zu verwirren, denn statt
selbst dem Prokuristen nachzulaufen oder wenigstens Gregor in der Verfolgung nicht zu hindern, packte er mit der
Rechten den Stock des Prokuristen, den dieser mit Hut und
Überzieher auf einem Sessel zurückgelassen hatte, holte mit
der Linken eine grosse Zeitung vom Tisch und machte
sich unter Füssestampfen daran, Gregor durch Schwenken
des Stockes und der Zeitung in sein Zimmer zurückzutreiben. Kein Bitten Gregors half, kein Bitten wurde auch
verstanden, er mochte den Kopf noch so demütig drehen,
der Vater stampfte nur stärker mit den Füssen. Drüben
hatte die Mutter trotz des kühlen Wetters ein Fenster aufgerissen, und hinausgelehnt drückte sie ihr Gesicht weit
ausserhalb des Fensters in ihre Hände. Zwischen Gasse und

"Help, for God's sake, help!" bent her head down as if to see Gregor better, yet on the contrary kept backing senselessly away; had quite forgotten that the laden table stood behind her; sat upon it hastily, as if in absence of mind, when she bumped into it; and seemed altogether unaware that the big coffee pot beside her was upset and pouring coffee in a flood over the carpet.

"Mother, Mother," said Gregor in a low voice, and looked up at her. The chief clerk, for the moment, had quite slipped from his mind; instead, he could not resist snapping his jaws together at the sight of the streaming coffee. That made his mother scream again, she fled from the table and fell into the arms of his father, who hastened to catch her. But Gregor had now no time to spare for his parents; the chief clerk was already on the stairs; with his chin on the banisters he was taking one last backward look. Gregor made a dash, to be as sure as possible of overtaking him; the chief clerk must have divined his intention, for he leaped down several steps and vanished; he was still yelling "Ugh!" and it echoed through the whole staircase. Unfortunately, the flight of the chief clerk seemed completely to upset Gregor's father, who had remained relatively calm until now, for instead of running after the man himself, or at least not hindering Gregor in his pursuit, he seized in his right hand the walking stick which the chief clerk had left behind on a chair, together with a hat and greatcoat, snatched in his left hand a large newspaper from the table and began stamping his feet and flourishing the stick and the newspaper to drive Gregor back into his room. No entreaty of Gregor's availed, indeed no entreaty was even understood, however humbly he bent his head his father only stamped on the floor the more loudly. Behind his father his mother had torn open a window, despite the cold weather, and was leaning far out of it with her face in her hands. A

Treppenhaus entstand eine starke Zugluft, die Fenstervor-
hänge flogen auf, die Zeitungen auf dem Tische rauschten,
einzelne Blätter wehten über den Boden hin. Unerbittlich
drängte der Vater und stiess Zischlaute aus, wie ein Wilder.
Nun hatte aber Gregor noch gar keine Übung im Rückwärts-
gehen, es ging wirklich sehr langsam. Wenn sich Gregor
nur hätte umdrehen dürfen, er wäre gleich in seinem Zimmer gewesen, aber er fürchtete sich, den Vater durch die
zeitraubende Umdrehung ungeduldig zu machen, und jeden Augenblick drohte ihm doch von dem Stock in des
Vaters Hand der tödliche Schlag auf den Rücken oder auf
den Kopf. Endlich aber blieb Gregor doch nichts anderes
übrig, denn er merkte mit Entsetzen, dass er im Rück-
wärtsgehen nicht einmal die Richtung einzuhalten verstand; und so begann er, unter unaufhörlichen ängstlichen
Seitenblicken nach dem Vater, sich nach Möglichkeit rasch,
in Wirklichkeit aber doch nur sehr langsam umzudrehen.
Vielleicht merkte der Vater seinen guten Willen, denn er
störte ihn hierbei nicht, sondern dirigierte sogar hie und
da die Drehbewegung von der Ferne mit der Spitze seines
Stockes. Wenn nur nicht dieses unerträgliche Zischen des
Vaters gewesen wäre! Gregor verlor darüber ganz den
Kopf. Er war schon fast ganz umgedreht, als er sich,
immer auf dieses Zischen horchend, sogar irrte und sich
wieder ein Stück zurückdrehte. Als er aber endlich glücklich mit dem Kopf vor der Türöffnung war, zeigte es sich,
dass sein Körper zu breit war, um ohne weiteres durchzu-
kommen. Dem Vater fiel es natürlich in seiner gegenwärtigen Verfassung auch nicht entfernt ein, etwa den anderen
Türflügel zu öffnen, um für Gregor einen genügenden
Durchgang zu schaffen. Seine fixe Idee war bloss, dass
Gregor so rasch als möglich in sein Zimmer müsse. Niemals
hätte er auch die umständlichen Vorbereitungen gestattet,
die Gregor brauchte, um sich aufzurichten und vielleicht
auf diese Weise durch die Tür zu kommen. Vielmehr trieb
er, als gäbe es kein Hindernis, Gregor jetzt unter besonderem Lärm vorwärts; es klang schon hinter Gregor gar

strong draught set in from the street to the staircase,
the window curtains blew in, the newspapers on the table
fluttered, stray pages whisked over the floor. Pitilessly
Gregor's father drove him back, hissing and crying
"Shoo!" like a savage. But Gregor was quite unpracticed
in walking backwards, it really was a slow business. If
he only had a chance to turn round he could get back
to his room at once, but he was afraid of exasperating
his father by the slowness of such a rotation and at any
moment the stick in his father's hand might hit him a
fatal blow on the back or on the head. In the end, however, nothing else was left for him to do since to his
horror he observed that in moving backwards he could
not even control the direction he took; and so, keeping
an anxious eye on his father all the time over his shoulder, he began to turn round as quickly as he could,
which was in reality very slowly. Perhaps his father
noted his good intentions, for he did not interfere except every now and then to help him in the maneuver
from a distance with the point of the stick. If only he
would have stopped making that unbearable hissing
noise! It made Gregor quite lose his head. He had turned
almost completely round when the hissing noise so dis-
tracted him that he even turned a little the wrong way
again. But when at last his head was fortunately right in
front of the doorway, it appeared that his body was too
broad simply to get through the opening. His father,
of course, in his present mood was far from thinking of
such a thing as opening the other half of the door, to
let Gregor have enough space. He had merely the fixed
idea of driving Gregor back into his room as quickly
as possible. He would never have suffered Gregor to
make the circumstantial preparations for standing up on
end and perhaps slipping this way through the door.
Rather, he was now making more noise than ever to
urge Gregor forward, as if no obstacle impeded him; to
Gregor, anyhow, the noise in his rear sounded no

nicht mehr wie die Stimme bloss eines einzigen Vaters; nun gab es wirklich keinen Spass mehr, und Gregor drängte sich — geschehe was wolle — in die Tür. Die eine Seite seines Körpers hob sich, er lag schief in der Türöffnung, seine eine Flanke war ganz wundgerieben, an der weissen Tür blieben hässliche Flecken, bald steckte er fest und hätte sich allein nicht mehr rühren können, die Beinchen auf der einen Seite hingen zitternd oben in der Luft, die auf der anderen waren schmerzhaft zu Boden gedrückt — da gab ihm der Vater von hinten einen jetzt wahrhaftig erlösenden starken Stoss, und er flog, heftig blutend, weit in sein Zimmer hinein. Die Tür wurde noch mit dem Stock zugeschlagen, dann war es endlich still.

II

ERST IN DER Abenddämmerung erwachte Gregor aus seinem schweren ohnmachtsähnlichen Schlaf. Er wäre gewiss nicht viel später auch ohne Störung erwacht, denn er fühlte sich genügend ausgeruht und ausgeschlafen, doch schien es ihm, als hätte ihn ein flüchtiger Schritt und ein vorsichtiges Schliessen der zum Vorzimmer führenden Tür geweckt. Der Schein der elektrischen Strassenlampen lag bleich hier und da auf der Zimmerdecke und auf den höheren Teilen der Möbel, aber unten bei Gregor war es finster. Langsam schob er sich, noch ungeschickt mit seinen Fühlern tastend, die er erst jetzt schätzen lernte, zur Türe hin, um nachzusehen, was dort geschehen war. Seine linke Seite schien eine einzige lange, unangenehm spannende Narbe, und er musste auf seinen zwei Beinreihen regelrecht hinken. Ein Beinchen war übrigens im Laufe der vormittägigen Vorfälle schwer verletzt worden — es war fast ein Wunder, dass ñur eines verletzt worden war — und schleppte leblos nach.

Erst bei der Tür merkte er, was ihn dorthin eigentlich gelockt hatte; es war der Geruch von etwas Essbarem ge-

longer like the voice of one single father; this was really no joke, and Gregor thrust himself—come what might—into the doorway. One side of his body rose up, he was tilted at an angle in the doorway, his flank was quite bruised, horrid blotches stained the white door, soon he was stuck fast and, left to himself, could not have moved at all, his legs on one side fluttered trembling in the air, those on the other were crushed painfully to the floor—when from behind his father gave him a strong push which was literally a deliverance and he flew far into the room, bleeding freely. The door was slammed behind him with the stick, and then at last there was silence.

II

Not until it was twilight did Gregor awake out of a deep sleep, more like a swoon than a sleep. He would certainly have waked up of his own accord not much later, for he felt himself sufficiently rested and well-slept, but it seemed to him as if a fleeting step and a cautious shutting of the door leading into the hall had aroused him. The electric lights in the street cast a pale sheen here and there on the ceiling and the upper surfaces of the furniture, but down below, where he lay, it was dark. Slowly, awkwardly trying out his feelers, which he only now learned to appreciate, he pushed his way to the door to see what had been happening there. His left side felt like one single long, unpleasantly tense scar, and he had actually to limp on his two rows of legs. One little leg, moreover, had been severely damaged in the course of that morning's events—it was almost a miracle that only one had been damaged—and trailed uselessly behind him.

He had reached the door before he discovered what had really drawn him to it: the smell of food. For there

wesen. Denn dort stand ein Napf mit süsser Milch gefüllt, in der kleine Schnitten von Weissbrot schwammen. Fast hätte er vor Freude gelacht, denn er hatte noch grösseren Hunger als am Morgen, und gleich tauchte er seinen Kopf fast bis über die Augen in die Milch hinein. Aber bald zog er ihn enttäuscht wieder zurück; nicht nur, dass ihm das Essen wegen seiner heiklen linken Seite Schwierigkeiten machte — und er konnte nur essen, wenn der ganze Körper schnaufend mitarbeitete —, so schmeckte ihm überdies die Milch, die sonst sein Lieblingsgetränk war und die ihm gewiss die Schwester deshalb hereingestellt hatte, gar nicht, ja er wandte sich fast mit Widerwillen von dem Napf ab und kroch in die Zimmermitte zurück.

Im Wohnzimmer war, wie Gregor durch die Türspalte sah, das Gas angezündet, aber während sonst zu dieser Tageszeit der Vater seine nachmittags erscheinende Zeitung der Mutter und manchmal auch der Schwester mit erhobener Stimme vorzulesen pflegte, hörte man jetzt keinen Laut. Nun vielleicht war dieses Vorlesen, von dem ihm die Schwester immer erzählte und schrieb, in der letzten Zeit überhaupt aus der Übung gekommen. Aber auch ringsherum war es so still, trotzdem doch gewiss die Wohnung nicht leer war. "Was für ein stilles Leben die Familie doch führte", sagte sich Gregor und fühlte, während er starr vor sich ins Dunkle sah, einen grossen Stolz darüber, dass er seinen Eltern und seiner Schwester ein solches Leben in einer so schönen Wohnung hatte verschaffen können. Wie aber, wenn jetzt alle Ruhe, aller Wohlstand, alle Zufriedenheit ein Ende mit Schrecken nehmen sollte? Um sich nicht in solche Gedanken zu verlieren, setzte sich Gregor lieber in Bewegung und kroch im Zimmer auf und ab.

Einmal während des langen Abends wurde die eine Seitentüre und einmal die andere bis zu einer kleinen Spalte geöffnet und rasch wieder geschlossen; jemand hatte wohl das Bedürfnis hereinzukommen, aber auch wieder zu viele Bedenken. Gregor machte nun unmittelbar bei der Wohnzimmertür Halt, entschlossen, den zögernden Besucher

stood a bowl filled with fresh milk in which floated
little sops of white bread. He could almost have laughed
with joy, since he was now still hungrier than in the
morning, and he dipped his head almost over the eyes
straight into the milk. But soon in disappointment he
withdrew it again; not only did he find it difficult to
feed because of his tender left side—and he could only
feed with the palpitating collaboration of his whole body
—he did not like the milk either, although milk had
been his favorite drink and that was certainly why his
sister had set it there for him, indeed it was almost with
repulsion that he turned away from the bowl and
crawled back to the middle of the room.

He could see through the crack of the door that the
gas was turned on in the living room, but while usually
at this time his father made a habit of reading the after-
noon newspaper in a loud voice to his mother and occa-
sionally to his sister as well, not a sound was now to be
heard. Well, perhaps his father had recently given up
this habit of reading aloud, which his sister had mentioned so often in conversation and in her letters. But
there was the same silence all around, although the flat
was certainly not empty of occupants. "What a quiet
life our family has been leading," said Gregor to himself, and as he sat there motionless staring into the darkness he felt great pride in the fact that he had been able
to provide such a life for his parents and sister in such a
fine flat. But what if all the quiet, the comfort, the con-
tentment were now to end in horror? To keep himself
from being lost in such thoughts Gregor took refuge in
movement and crawled up and down the room.

Once during the long evening one of the side doors
was opened a little and quickly shut again, later the
other side door too; someone had apparently wanted to
come in and then thought better of it. Gregor now
stationed himself immediately before the living-room
door, determined to persuade any hesitating visitor to

doch irgendwie hereinzubringen oder doch wenigstens zu erfahren, wer es sei; aber nun wurde die Tür nicht mehr geöffnet und Gregor wartete vergebens. Früh, als die Türen versperrt waren, hatten alle zu ihm hereinkommen wollen, jetzt, da er die eine Tür geöffnet hatte und die anderen offenbar während des Tages geöffnet worden waren, kam keiner mehr, und die Schlüssel steckten nun auch von aussen.

Spät erst in der Nacht wurde das Licht im Wohnzimmer ausgelöscht, und nun war leicht festzustellen, dass die Eltern und die Schwester so lange wachgeblieben waren, denn wie man genau hören konnte, entfernten sich jetzt alle drei auf den Fusspitzen. Nun kam gewiss bis zum Morgen niemand mehr zu Gregor herein; er hatte also eine lange Zeit, um ungestört zu überlegen, wie er sein Leben jetzt neu ordnen sollte. Aber das hohe freie Zimmer, in dem er gezwungen war, flach auf dem Boden zu liegen, ängstigte ihn, ohne dass er die Ursache herausfinden konnte, denn es war ja sein seit fünf Jahren von ihm bewohntes Zimmer — und mit einer halb unbewussten Wendung und nicht ohne eine leichte Scham eilte er unter das Kanapee, wo er sich, trotzdem sein Rücken ein wenig gedrückt wurde und trotzdem er den Kopf nicht mehr erheben konnte, gleich sehr behaglich fühlte und nur bedauerte, dass sein Körper zu breit war, um vollständig unter dem Kanapee untergebracht zu werden.

Dort blieb er die ganze Nacht, die er zum Teil im Halbschlaf, aus dem ihn der Hunger immer wieder aufschreckte, verbrachte, zum Teil aber in Sorgen und undeutlichen Hoffnungen, die aber alle zu dem Schlusse führten, dass er sich vorläufig ruhig verhalten und durch Geduld und grösste Rücksichtnahme der Familie die Unannehmlichkeiten erträglich machen müsse, die er ihr in seinem gegenwärtigen Zustand nun einmal zu verursachen gezwungen war.

Schon am frühen Morgen, es war fast noch Nacht, hatte Gregor Gelegenheit, die Kraft seiner eben gefassten Ent-

come in or at least to discover who it might be; but the door was not opened again and he waited in vain. In the early morning, when the doors were locked, they had all wanted to come in, now that he had opened one door and the other had apparently been opened during the day, no one came in and even the keys were on the other side of the doors.

It was late at night before the gas went out in the living room, and Gregor could easily tell that his parents and his sister had all stayed awake until then, for he could clearly hear the three of them stealing away on tiptoe. No one was likely to visit him, not until the morning, that was certain; so he had plenty of time to meditate at his leisure on how he was to arrange his life afresh. But the lofty, empty room in which he had to lie flat on the floor filled him with an apprehension he could not account for, since it had been his very own room for the past five years—and with a half-unconscious action, not without a slight feeling of shame, he scuttled under the sofa, where he felt comfortable at once, although his back was a little cramped and he could not lift his head up, and his only regret was that his body was too broad to get the whole of it under the sofa.

He stayed there all night, spending the time partly in a light slumber, from which his hunger kept waking him up with a start, and partly in worrying and sketching vague hopes, which all led to the same conclusion, that he must lie low for the present and, by exercising patience and the utmost consideration, help the family to bear the inconvenience he was bound to cause them in his present condition.

Very early in the morning, it was still almost night, Gregor had the chance to test the strength of his new

schlüsse zu prüfen, denn vom Vorzimmer her öffnete die Schwester, fast völlig angezogen, die Tür und sah mit Spannung herein. Sie fand ihn nicht gleich, aber als sie ihn unter dem Kanapee bemerkte — Gott, er musste doch irgendwo sein, er hatte doch nicht wegfliegen können — erschrak sie so sehr, dass sie, ohne sich beherrschen zu können, die Tür von aussen wieder zuschlug. Aber als bereue sie ihr Benehmen, öffnete sie die Tür sofort wieder und trat, als sei sie bei einem Schwerkranken oder gar bei einem Fremden, auf den Fusspitzen herein. Gregor hatte den Kopf bis knapp zum Rande des Kanapees vorgeschoben und beobachtete sie. Ob sie wohl bemerken würde, dass er die Milch stehen gelassen hatte, und zwar keineswegs aus Mangel an Hunger, und ob sie eine andere Speise hereinbringen würde, die ihm besser entsprach? Täte sie es nicht von selbst, er wollte lieber verhungern, als sie darauf aufmerksam machen, trotzdem es ihn eigentlich ungeheuer drängte, unterm Kanapee vorzuschiessen, sich der Schwester zu Füssen zu werfen und sie um irgend etwas Gutes zum Essen zu bitten. Aber die Schwester bemerkte sofort mit Verwunderung den noch vollen Napf, aus dem nur ein wenig Milch ringsherum verschüttet war, sie hob ihn gleich auf, zwar nicht mit den blossen Händen, sondern mit einem Fetzen, und trug ihn hinaus. Gregor war äusserst neugierig was sie zum Ersatze bringen würde, und er machte sich die verschiedensten Gedanken darüber. Niemals aber hätte er erraten können, was die Schwester in ihrer Güte wirklich tat. Sie brachte ihm, um seinen Geschmack zu prüfen, eine ganze Auswahl, alles auf einer alten Zeitung ausgebreitet. Da war altes halbverfaultes Gemüse; Knochen vom Nachtmahl her, die von festgewordener weisser Sauce umgeben waren; ein paar Rosinen und Mandeln; ein Käse, den Gregor vor zwei Tagen für ungeniessbar erklärt hatte; ein trockenes Brot, ein mit Butter beschmiertes Brot und ein mit Butter beschmiertes und gesalzenes Brot. Ausserdem stellte sie zu dem allen noch den wahrscheinlich ein für allemal für Gregor bestimmten Napf, in den sie Wasser

resolutions, for his sister, nearly fully dressed, opened the door from the hall and peered in. She did not see him at once, yet when she caught sight of him under the sofa—well, he had to be somewhere, he couldn't have flown away, could he?—she was so startled that without being able to help it she slammed the door shut again. But as if regretting her behavior she opened the door again immediately and came in on tiptoe, as if she were visiting an invalid or even a stranger. Gregor had pushed his head forward to the very edge of the sofa and watched her. Would she notice that he had left the milk standing, and not for lack of hunger, and would she bring in some other kind of food more to his taste? If she did not do it of her own accord, he would rather starve than draw her attention to the fact, although he felt a wild impulse to dart out from under the sofa, throw himself at her feet and beg her for something to eat. But his sister at once noticed, with surprise, that the bowl was still full, except for a little milk that had been spilt all around it, she lifted it immediately, not with her bare hands, true, but with a cloth and carried it away. Gregor was wildly curious to know what she would bring instead, and made various speculations about it. Yet what she actually did next, in the goodness of her heart, he could never have guessed at. To find out what he liked she brought him a whole selection of food, all set out on an old newspaper. There were old, half-decayed vegetables, bones from last night's supper covered with a white sauce that had thickened; some raisins and almonds; a piece of cheese that Gregor would have called uneatable two days ago; a dry roll of bread, a buttered roll, and a roll both buttered and salted. Besides all that, she set down again the same bowl, into which she had poured some water, and which was apparently to be reserved for his exclusive use. And with fine tact, knowing that Gregor would not eat in her presence, she withdrew quickly and even turned the

gegossen hatte. Und aus Zartgefühl, da sie wusste, dass Gregor vor ihr nicht essen würde, entfernte sie sich eiligst und drehte sogar den Schlüssel um, damit nur Gregor merken könne, dass er es sich so behaglich machen dürfe, wie er wolle. Gregors Beinchen schwirrten, als es jetzt zum Essen ging. Seine Wunden mussten übrigens auch schon vollständig geheilt sein, er fühlte keine Behinderung mehr, er staunte darüber und dachte daran, wie er vor mehr als einem Monat sich mit dem Messer ganz wenig in den Finger geschnitten, und wie ihm diese Wunde noch vorgestern genug wehgetan hatte. Sollte ich jetzt weniger Feingefühl haben? dachte er und saugte schon gierig an dem Käse, zu dem es ihn vor allen anderen Speisen sofort und nachdrücklich gezogen hatte. Rasch hintereinander und mit vor Befriedigung tränenden Augen verzehrte er den Käse, das Gemüse und die Sauce; die frischen Speisen dagegen schmeckten ihm nicht, er konnte nicht einmal ihren Geruch vertragen und schleppte sogar die Sachen, die er essen wollte, ein Stückchen weiter weg. Er war schon längst mit allem fertig und lag nur noch faul auf der gleichen Stelle, als die Schwester zum Zeichen, dass er sich zurückziehen solle, langsam den Schlüssel umdrehte. Das schreckte ihn sofort auf, trotzdem er schon fast schlummerte, und er eilte wieder unter das Kanapee. Aber es kostete ihn grosse Selbstüberwindung, auch nur die kurze Zeit, während welcher die Schwester im Zimmer war, unter dem Kanapee zu bleiben, denn von dem reichlichen Essen hatte sich sein Leib ein wenig gerundet, und er konnte dort in der Enge kaum atmen. Unter kleinen Erstickungsanfällen sah er mit etwas hervorgequollenen Augen zu, wie die nichtsahnende Schwester mit einem Besen nicht nur die Überbleibsel zusammenkehrte, sondern selbst die von Gregor gar nicht berührten Speisen, als seien also auch diese nicht mehr zu gebrauchen, und wie sie alles hastig in einen Kübel schüttete, den sie mit einem Holzdeckel schloss, worauf sie alles hinaustrug. Kaum hatte sie sich umgedreht, zog sich schon Gregor unter dem Kanapee hervor und streckte und blähte sich.

key, to let him understand that he could take his ease
as much as he liked. Gregor's legs all whizzed towards
the food. His wounds must have healed completely,
moreover, for he felt no disability, which amazed him
and made him reflect how more than a month ago he had
cut one finger a little with a knife and had still suffered
pain from the wound only the day before yesterday.
Am I less sensitive now? he thought, and sucked greedily
at the cheese, which above all the other edibles attracted
him at once and strongly. One after another and with
tears of satisfaction in his eyes he quickly devoured the
cheese, the vegetables and the sauce; the fresh food, on
the other hand, had no charms for him, he could not
even stand the smell of it and actually dragged away to
some little distance the things he could eat. He had
long finished his meal and was only lying lazily on
the same spot when his sister turned the key slowly as
a sign for him to retreat. That roused him at once, although he was nearly asleep, and he hurried under the
sofa again. But it took considerable self-control for him
to stay under the sofa, even for the short time his sister
was in the room, since the large meal had swollen his
body somewhat and he was so cramped he could hardly
breathe. Slight attacks of breathlessness afflicted him and
his eyes were starting a little out of his head as he
watched his unsuspecting sister sweeping together with
a broom not only the remains of what he had eaten but
even the things he had not touched, as if these were now
of no use to anyone, and hastily shoveling it all into a
bucket, which she covered with a wooden lid and carried away. Hardly had she turned her back when
Gregor came from under the sofa and stretched and
puffed himself out.

Auf diese Weise bekam nun Gregor täglich sein Essen, einmal am Morgen, wenn die Eltern und das Dienstmädchen noch schliefen, das zweitemal nach dem allgemeinen Mittagessen, denn dann schliefen die Eltern gleichfalls noch ein Weilchen, und das Dienstmädchen wurde von der Schwester mit irgendeiner Besorgung weggeschickt. Gewiss wollten auch sie nicht, dass Gregor verhungere, aber vielleicht hätten sie es nicht ertragen können, von seinem Essen mehr als durch Hörensagen zu erfahren, vielleicht wollte die Schwester ihnen auch eine möglicherweise nur kleine Trauer ersparen, denn tatsächlich litten sie ja gerade genug.

Mit welchen Ausreden man an jenem ersten Vormittag den Arzt und den Schlosser wieder aus der Wohnung geschafft hatte, konnte Gregor gar nicht erfahren, denn da er nicht verstanden wurde, dachte niemand daran, auch die Schwester nicht, dass er die anderen verstehen könne, und so musste er sich, wenn die Schwester in seinem Zimmer war, damit begnügen, nur hier und da ihre Seufzer und Anrufe der Heiligen zu hören. Erst später, als sie sich ein wenig an alles gewöhnt hatte — von vollständiger Gewöhnung konnte natürlich niemals die Rede sein —, erhaschte Gregor manchmal eine Bemerkung, die freundlich gemeint war oder so gedeutet werden konnte. "Heute hat es ihm aber geschmeckt", sagte sie, wenn Gregor unter dem Essen tüchtig aufgeräumt hatte, während sie im gegenteiligen Fall, der sich allmählich immer häufiger wiederholte, fast traurig zu sagen pflegte: "Nun ist wieder alles stehengeblieben."

Während aber Gregor unmittelbar keine Neuigkeit erfahren konnte, erhorchte er manches aus den Nebenzimmern, und wo er nur einmal Stimmen hörte, lief er gleich zu der betreffenden Tür und drückte sich mit ganzem Leib an sie. Besonders in der ersten Zeit gab es kein Gespräch, das nicht irgendwie, wenn auch nur im geheimen, von ihm handelte. Zwei Tage lang waren bei allen Mahlzeiten Beratungen darüber zu hören, wie man sich jetzt verhalten solle; aber auch zwischen den Mahlzeiten sprach

In this manner Gregor was fed, once in the early morning while his parents and the servant girl were still asleep, and a second time after they had all had their midday dinner, for then his parents took a short nap and the servant girl could be sent out on some errand or other by his sister. Not that they would have wanted him to starve, of course, but perhaps they could not have borne to know more about his feeding than from hearsay, perhaps too his sister wanted to spare them such little anxieties wherever possible, since they had quite enough to bear as it was.

Under what pretext the doctor and the locksmith had been got rid of on that first morning Gregor could not discover, for since what he said was not understood by the others it never struck any of them, not even his sister, that he could understand what they said, and so whenever his sister came into his room he had to content himself with hearing her utter only a sigh now and then and an occasional appeal to the saints. Later on, when she had got a little used to the situation—of course she could never get completely used to it—she sometimes threw out a remark which was kindly meant or could be so interpreted. "Well, he liked his dinner today," she would say when Gregor had made a good clearance of his food; and when he had not eaten, which gradually happened more and more often, she would say almost sadly: "Everything's been left standing again."

But although Gregor could get no news directly, he overheard a lot from the neighboring rooms, and as soon as voices were audible, he would run to the door of the room concerned and press his whole body against it. In the first few days especially there was no conversation that did not refer to him somehow, even if only indirectly. For two whole days there were family consultations at every mealtime about what should be done; but also between meals the same subject was discussed,

man über das gleiche Thema, denn immer waren zumindest zwei Familienmitglieder zu Hause, da wohl niemand allein zu Hause bleiben wollte und man die Wohnung doch auf keinen Fall gänzlich verlassen konnte. Auch hatte das Dienstmädchen gleich am ersten Tag — es war nicht ganz klar, was und wieviel sie von dem Vorgefallenen wusste — kniefällig die Mutter gebeten, sie sofort zu entlassen, und als sie sich eine Viertelstunde danach verabschiedete, dankte sie für die Entlassung unter Tränen, wie für die grösste Wohltat, die man ihr hier erwiesen hatte, und gab, ohne dass man es von ihr verlangte, einen fürchterlichen Schwur ab, niemandem auch nur das geringste zu verraten.

Nun musste die Schwester im Verein mit der Mutter auch kochen; allerdings machte das nicht viel Mühe, denn man ass fast nichts. Immer wieder hörte Gregor, wie der eine den anderen vergebens zum Essen aufforderte und keine andere Antwort bekam, als: "Danke, ich habe genug" oder etwas Ähnliches. Getrunken wurde vielleicht auch nichts. Öfters fragte die Schwester den Vater, ob er Bier haben wolle, und herzlich erbot sie sich, es selbst zu holen, und als der Vater schwieg, sagte sie, um ihm jedes Bedenken zu nehmen, sie könne auch die Hausmeisterin darum schicken, aber dann sagte der Vater schliesslich ein grosses "Nein", und es wurde nicht mehr davon gesprochen.

Schon im Laufe des ersten Tages legte der Vater die ganzen Vermögensverhältnisse und Aussichten sowohl der Mutter als auch der Schwester dar. Hie und da stand er vom Tische auf und holte aus seiner kleinen Wertheimkassa, die er aus dem vor fünf Jahren erfolgten Zusammenbruch seines Geschäftes gerettet hatte, irgendeinen Beleg oder irgendein Vormerkbuch. Man hörte, wie er das komplizierte Schloss aufsperrte und nach Entnahme des Gesuchten wieder verschloss. Diese Erklärungen des Vaters waren zum Teil das erste Erfreuliche, was Gregor seit seiner Gefangenschaft zu hören bekam. Er war der Meinung gewesen, dass dem Vater von jenem Geschäft her nicht das Geringste übriggeblieben war, zumindest hatte ihm

for there were always at least two members of the family at home, since no one wanted to be alone in the flat and to leave it quite empty was unthinkable. And on the very first of these days the household cook—it was not quite clear what and how much she knew of the situation— went down on her knees to his mother and begged leave to go, and when she departed, a quarter of an hour later, gave thanks for her dismissal with tears in her eyes as if for the greatest benefit that could have been conferred on her, and without any prompting swore a solemn oath that she would never say a single word to anyone about what had happened.

Now Gregor's sister had to cook too, helping her mother; true, the cooking did not amount to much, for they ate scarcely anything. Gregor was always hearing one of the family vainly urging another to eat and getting no answer but: "Thanks, I've had all I want," or something similar. Perhaps they drank nothing either. Time and again his sister kept asking his father if he wouldn't like some beer and offered kindly to go and fetch it herself, and when he made no answer suggested that she could ask the concierge to fetch it, so that he need feel no sense of obligation, but then a round "No" came from his father and no more was said about it.

In the course of that very first day Gregor's father explained the family's financial position and prospects to both his mother and his sister. Now and then he rose from the table to get some voucher or memorandum out of the small safe he had rescued from the collapse of his business five years earlier. One could hear him opening the complicated lock and rustling papers out and shutting it again. This statement made by his father was the first cheerful information Gregor had heard since his imprisonment. He had been of the opinion that nothing at all was left over from his father's business, at least his father had never said anything to the contrary, and of course he had not asked him directly. At that

der Vater nichts Gegenteiliges gesagt, und Gregor allerdings hatte ihn auch nicht darum gefragt. Gregors Sorge
war damals nur gewesen, alles daranzusetzen, um die Familie das geschäftliche Unglück, das alle in eine vollstän-
dige Hoffnungslosigkeit gebracht hatte, möglichst rasch
vergessen zu lassen. Und so hatte er damals mit ganz
besonderem Feuer zu arbeiten angefangen und war fast
über Nacht aus einem kleinen Kommis ein Reisender geworden, der natürlich ganz andere Möglichkeiten des
Geldverdienens hatte, und dessen Arbeitserfolge sich sofort
in Form der Provision zu Bargeld verwandelten, das der
erstaunten und beglückten Familie zu Hause auf den Tisch
gelegt werden konnte. Es waren schöne Zeiten gewesen,
und niemals nachher hatten sie sich, wenigstens in diesem
Glanze, wiederholt, trotzdem Gregor später so viel Geld
verdiente, dass er den Aufwand der ganzen Familie zu
tragen imstande war und auch trug. Man hatte sich eben
daran gewöhnt, sowohl die Familie als auch Gregor, man
nahm das Geld dankbar an, er lieferte es gern ab, aber eine
besondere Wärme wollte sich nicht mehr ergeben. Nur
die Schwester war Gregor doch noch nahe geblieben, und
es war sein geheimer Plan, sie, die zum Unterschied von
Gregor Musik sehr liebte und rührend Violine zu spielen
verstand, nächstes Jahr, ohne Rücksicht auf die grossen
Kosten, die das verursachen musste, und die man schon
auf andere Weise hereinbringen würde, auf das Konservatorium zu schicken. Öfters während der kurzen Aufenthalte
Gregors in der Stadt wurde in den Gesprächen mit der
Schwester das Konservatorium erwähnt, aber immer nur
als schöner Traum, an dessen Verwirklichung nicht zu
denken war, und die Eltern hörten nicht einmal diese
unschuldigen Erwähnungen gern; aber Gregor dachte sehr
bestimmt daran und beabsichtigte, es am Weihnachtsabend
feierlich zu erklären.

Solche in seinem gegenwärtigen Zustand ganz nutzlose
Gedanken gingen ihm durch den Kopf, während er dort
aufrecht an der Türe klebte und horchte. Manchmal konnte

time Gregor's sole desire was to do his utmost to help
the family to forget as soon as possible the catastrophe
which had overwhelmed the business and thrown them
all into a state of complete despair. And so he had set
to work with unusual ardor and almost overnight had
become a commercial traveler instead of a little clerk,
with of course much greater chances of earning money,
and his success was immediately translated into good
round coin which he could lay on the table for his
amazed and happy family. These had been fine times,
and they had never recurred, at least not with the same
sense of glory, although later on Gregor had earned so
much money that he was able to meet the expenses of
the whole household and did so. They had simply got
used to it, both the family and Gregor; the money was
gratefully accepted and gladly given, but there was no
special uprush of warm feeling. With his sister alone had
he remained intimate, and it was a secret plan of his that
she, who loved music, unlike himself, and could play
movingly on the violin, should be sent next year to
study at the Conservatorium, despite the great expense
that would entail, which must be made up in some other
way. During his brief visits home the Conservatorium
was often mentioned in the talks he had with his sister,
but always merely as a beautiful dream which could
never come true, and his parents discouraged even these
innocent references to it; yet Gregor had made up his
mind firmly about it and meant to announce the fact
with due solemnity on Christmas Day.

Such were the thoughts, completely futile in his present condition, that went through his head as he stood
clinging upright to the door and listening. Sometimes

er vor allgemeiner Müdigkeit gar nicht mehr zuhören und
liess den Kopf nachlässig gegen die Tür schlagen, hielt ihn
aber sofort wieder fest, denn selbst das kleine Geräusch,
das er damit verursacht hatte, war nebenan gehört worden
und hatte alle verstummen lassen. "Was er nur wieder
treibt", sagte der Vater nach einer Weile, offenbar zur
Türe hingewendet, und dann erst wurde das unterbrochene
Gespräch allmählich wieder aufgenommen.

Gregor erfuhr nun zur Genüge — denn der Vater
pflegte sich in seinen Erklärungen öfters zu wiederholen,
teils, weil er selbst sich mit diesen Dingen schon lange
nicht beschäftigt hatte, teils auch, weil die Mutter nicht
alles gleich beim erstenmal verstand —, dass trotz allen
Unglücks ein allerdings ganz kleines Vermögen aus der
alten Zeit noch vorhanden war, das die nicht angerührten
Zinsen in der Zwischenzeit ein wenig hatten anwachsen
lassen. Ausserdem aber war das Geld, das Gregor allmonat-
lich nach Hause gebracht hatte — er selbst hatte nur ein
paar Gulden für sich behalten·—, nicht vollständig aufge-
braucht worden und hatte sich zu einem kleinen Kapital
angesammelt. Gregor, hinter seiner Türe, nickte eifrig, er-
freut über diese unerwartete Vorsicht und Sparsamkeit.
Eigentlich hätte er ja mit diesen überschüssigen Geldern
die Schuld des Vaters gegenüber dem Chef weiter abge-
tragen haben können, und jener Tag, an dem er diesen
Posten hätte loswerden können, wäre weit näher gewesen,
aber jetzt war es zweifellos besser so, wie es der Vater ein-
gerichtet hatte.

Nun genügte dieses Geld aber ganz und gar nicht, um
die Familie etwa von den Zinsen leben zu lassen; es genügte
vielleicht, um die Familie ein, höchstens zwei Jahre zu erhalten, mehr war es nicht. Es war also bloss eine Summe,
die man eigentlich nicht angreifen durfte, und die für den
Notfall zurückgelegt werden musste; das Geld zum Leben
aber musste man verdienen. Nun war aber der Vater ein
zwar gesunder, aber alter Mann, der schon fünf Jahre

out of sheer weariness he had to give up listening and let his head fall negligently against the door, but he always had to pull himself together again at once, for even the slight sound his head made was audible next door and brought all conversation to a stop. "What can he be doing now?" his father would say after a while, obviously turning towards the door, and only then would the interrupted conversation gradually be set going again.

Gregor was now informed as amply as he could wish —for his father tended to repeat himself in his explanations, partly because it was a long time since he had handled such matters and partly because his mother could not always grasp things at once—that a certain amount of investments, a very small amount it was true, had survived the wreck of their fortunes and had even increased a little because the dividends had not been touched meanwhile. And besides that, the money Gregor brought home every month—he had kept only a few dollars for himself—had never been quite used up and now amounted to a small capital sum. Behind the door Gregor nodded his head eagerly, rejoiced at this evidence of unexpected thrift and foresight. True, he could really have paid off some more of his father's debts to the chief with this extra money, and so brought much nearer the day on which he could quit his job, but doubtless it was better the way his father had arranged it.

Yet this capital was by no means sufficient to let the family live on the interest of it; for one year, perhaps, or at the most two, they could live on the principal, that was all. It was simply a sum that ought not to be touched and should be kept for a rainy day; money for living expenses would have to be earned. Now his father was still hale enough but an old man, and he had done no work for the past five years and could not be expected

nichts gearbeitet hatte und sich jedenfalls nicht viel zu-
trauen durfte; er hatte in diesen fünf Jahren, welche die
ersten Ferien seines mühevollen und doch erfolglosen Lebens waren, viel Fett angesetzt und war dadurch recht
schwerfällig geworden. Und die alte Mutter sollte nun
vielleicht Geld verdienen, die an Asthma litt, der eine
Wanderung durch die Wohnung schon Anstrengung verursachte, und die jeden zweiten Tag in Atembeschwerden
auf dem Sofa beim offenen Fenster verbrachte? Und die
Schwester sollte Geld verdienen, die noch ein Kind war
mit ihren siebzehn Jahren, und der ihre bisherige Lebens-
weise so sehr zu gönnen war, die daraus bestanden hatte,
sich nett zu kleiden, lange zu schlafen, in der Wirtschaft
mitzuhelfen, an ein paar bescheidenen Vergnügungen sich
zu beteiligen und vor allem Violine zu spielen? Wenn die
Rede auf diese Notwendigkeit des Geldverdienens kam,
liess zuerst immer Gregor die Türe los und warf sich auf
das neben der Tür befindliche kühle Ledersofa, denn ihm
war ganz heiss vor Beschämung und Trauer.

Oft lag er dort die ganzen langen Nächte über, schlief
keinen Augenblick und scharrte nur stundenlang auf dem
Leder. Oder er scheute nicht die grosse Mühe, einen Sessel
zum Fenster zu schieben, dann die Fensterbrüstung hin-
aufzukriechen und, in den Sessel gestemmt, sich ans Fenster
zu lehnen, offenbar nur in irgendeiner Erinnerung an das
Befreiende, das früher für ihn darin gelegen war, aus dem
Fenster zu schauen. Denn tatsächlich sah er von Tag zu
Tag die auch nur ein wenig entfernten Dinge immer un-
deutlicher; das gegenüberliegende Krankenhaus, dessen nur
allzu häufigen Anblick er früher verflucht hatte, bekam er
überhaupt nicht mehr zu Gesicht, und wenn er nicht
genau gewusst hätte, dass er in der stillen, aber völlig
städtischen Charlottenstrasse wohnte, hätte er glauben können, von seinem Fenster aus in eine Einöde zu schauen, in
welcher der graue Himmel und die graue Erde ununter-
scheidbar sich vereinigten. Nur zweimal hatte die aufmerk-
same Schwester sehen müssen, dass der Sessel beim Fenster

to do much; during these five years, the first years of
leisure in his laborious though unsuccessful life, he had
grown rather fat and become sluggish. And Gregor's
old mother, how was she to earn a living with her
asthma, which troubled her even when she walked
through the flat and kept her lying on a sofa every other
day panting for breath beside an open window? And
was his sister to earn her bread, she who was still a child
of seventeen and whose life hitherto had been so pleas-
ant, consisting as it did in dressing herself nicely, sleeping long, helping in the housekeeping, going out to a
few modest entertainments and above all playing the
violin? At first whenever the need for earning money
was mentioned Gregor let go his hold on the door and
threw himself down on the cool leather sofa beside it, he
felt so hot with shame and grief.

Often he just lay there the long nights through without sleeping at all, scrabbling for hours on the leather.
Or he nerved himself to the great effort of pushing an
armchair to the window, then crawled up over the
window sill and, braced against the chair, leaned against
the window panes, obviously in some recollection of the
sense of freedom that looking out of a window always
used to give him. For in reality day by day things that
were even a little way off were growing dimmer to his
sight; the hospital across the street, which he used to
execrate for being all too often before his eyes, was now
quite beyond his range of vision, and if he had not
known that he lived in Charlotte Street, a quiet street
but still a city street, he might have believed that his
window gave on a desert waste where gray sky and gray
land blended indistinguishably into each other. His
quick-witted sister only needed to observe twice that
the armchair stood by the window; after that whenever

stand, als sie schon jedesmal, nachdem sie das Zimmer aufgeräumt hatte, den Sessel wieder genau zum Fenster hinschob, ja sogar von nun ab den inneren Fensterflügel offen liess.

Hätte Gregor nur mit der Schwester sprechen und ihr für alles danken können, was sie für ihn machen musste, er hätte ihre Dienste leichter ertragen; so aber litt er darunter. Die Schwester suchte freilich die Peinlichkeit des Ganzen zu verwischen, und je längere Zeit verging, desto besser gelang es ihr natürlich auch, aber auch Gregor durchschaute mit der Zeit alles viel genauer. Schon ihr Eintritt war für ihn schrecklich. Kaum war sie eingetreten, lief sie, ohne sich Zeit zu nehmen, die Türe zu schliessen, so sehr sie sonst darauf achtete, jedem den Anblick von Gregors Zimmer zu ersparen, geradewegs zum Fenster und riss es, als ersticke sie fast, mit hastigen Händen auf, blieb auch, selbst wenn es noch so kalt war, ein Weilchen beim Fenster und atmete tief. Mit diesem Laufen und Lärmen erschreckte sie Gregor täglich zweimal; die ganze Zeit über zitterte er unter dem Kanapee und wusste doch sehr gut, dass sie ihn gewiss gerne damit verschont hätte, wenn es ihr nur möglich gewesen wäre, sich in einem Zimmer, in dem sich Gregor befand, bei geschlossenem Fenster aufzuhalten.

Einmal, es war wohl schon ein Monat seit Gregors Verwandlung vergangen, und es war doch schon für die Schwester kein besonderer Grund mehr, über Gregors Aussehen in Erstaunen zu geraten, kam sie ein wenig früher als sonst und traf Gregor noch an, wie er, unbeweglich und so recht zum Erschrecken aufgestellt, aus dem Fenster schaute. Es wäre für Gregor nicht unerwartet gewesen, wenn sie nicht eingetreten wäre, da er sie durch seine Stellung verhinderte, sofort das Fenster zu öffnen, aber sie trat nicht nur nicht ein, sie fuhr sogar zurück und schloss die Tür; ein Fremder hätte geradezu denken können, Gregor habe ihr aufgelauert und habe sie beissen wollen. Gregor versteckte sich natürlich sofort unter dem

she had tidied the room she always pushed the chair
back to the same place at the window and even left
the inner casements open.

If he could have spoken to her and thanked her for
all she had to do for him, he could have borne her minis-
trations better; as it was, they oppressed him. She certainly tried to make as light as possible of whatever was
disagreeable in her task, and as time went on she succeeded, of course, more and more, but time brought
more enlightenment to Gregor too. The very way she
came in distressed him. Hardly was she in the room
when she rushed to the window, without even taking
time to shut the door, careful as she was usually to shield
the sight of Gregor's room from the others, and as if
she were almost suffocating tore the casements open
with hasty fingers, standing then in the open draught
for a while even in the bitterest cold and drawing deep
breaths. This noisy scurry of hers upset Gregor twice
a day; he would crouch trembling under the sofa all
the time, knowing quite well that she would certainly
have spared him such a disturbance had she found it at
all possible to stay in his presence without opening the
window.

On one occasion, about a month after Gregor's meta-
morphosis, when there was surely no reason for her
to be still startled at his appearance, she came a little
earlier than usual and found him gazing out of the
window, quite motionless, and thus well placed to look
like a bogey. Gregor would not have been surprised
had she not come in at all, for she could not immediately open the window while he was there, but not only
did she retreat, she jumped back as if in alarm and
banged the door shut; a stranger might well have
thought that he had been lying in wait for her there
meaning to bite her. Of course he hid himself under the
sofa at once, but he had to wait until midday before

Kanapee, aber er musste bis zum Mittag warten, ehe die Schwester wiederkam, und sie schien viel unruhiger als sonst. Er erkannte daraus, dass ihr sein Anblick noch immer unerträglich war und ihr auch weiterhin unerträglich bleiben müsse, und dass sie sich wohl sehr überwinden musste, vor dem Anblick auch nur der kleinen Partie seines Körpers nicht davonzulaufen, mit der er unter dem Kanapee hervorragte. Um ihr auch diesen Anblick zu ersparen, trug er eines Tages auf seinem Rücken — er brauchte zu dieser Arbeit vier Stunden — das Leintuch auf das Kanapee und ordnete es in einer solchen Weise an, dass er nun gänzlich verdeckt war, und dass die Schwester, selbst wenn sie sich bückte, ihn nicht sehen konnte. Wäre dieses Leintuch ihrer Meinung nach nicht nötig gewesen, dann hätte sie es ja entfernen können, denn dass es nicht zum Vergnügen Gregors gehören konnte, sich so ganz und gar abzusperren, war doch klar genug, aber sie liess das Leintuch, so wie es war, und Gregor glaubte sogar einen dankbaren Blick erhascht zu haben, als er einmal mit dem Kopf vorsichtig das Leintuch ein wenig lüftete, um nachzusehen, wie die Schwester die neue Einrichtung aufnahm.

In den ersten vierzehn Tagen konnten ·es die Eltern nicht über sich bringen, zu ihm hereinzukommen, und er hörte oft, wie sie die jetzige Arbeit der Schwester völlig anerkannten, während sie sich bisher häufig über die Schwester geärgert hatten, weil sie ihnen als ein etwas nutzloses Mädchen erschienen war. Nun aber warteten oft beide, der Vater und die Mutter, vor Gregors Zimmer, während die Schwester dort aufräumte, und kaum war sie herausgekommen, musste sie ganz genau erzählen, wie es in dem Zimmer aussah, was Gregor gegessen hatte, wie er sich diesmal benommen hatte, und ob vielleicht eine kleine Besserung zu bemerken war. Die Mutter übrigens wollte verhältnismässig bald Gregor besuchen, aber der Vater und die Schwester hielten sie zuerst mit Vernunftgründen zurück, denen Gregor sehr aufmerksam zuhörte, und die er vollständig billigte. Später aber musste man sie mit Gewalt

she came again, and she seemed more ill at ease than usual. This made him realize how repulsive the sight of him still was to her, and that it was bound to go on being repulsive, and what an effort it must cost her not to run away even from the sight of the small portion of his body that stuck out from under the sofa. In order to spare her that, therefore, one day he carried a sheet on his back to the sofa—it cost him four hours' labor— and arranged it there in such a way as to hide him completely, so that even if she were to bend down she could not see him. Had she considered the sheet unnecessary, she would certainly have stripped it off the sofa again, for it was clear enough that this curtaining and confining of himself was not likely to conduce to Gregor's comfort, but she left it where it was, and Gregor even fancied that he caught a thankful glance from her eye when he lifted the sheet carefully a very little with his head to see how she was taking the new arrangement.

For the first fortnight his parents could not bring themselves to the point of entering his room, and he often heard them expressing their appreciation of his sister's activities, whereas formerly they had frequently scolded her for being as they thought a somewhat useless daughter. But now, both of them often waited outside the door, his father and his mother, while his sister tidied his room, and as soon as she came out she had to tell them exactly how things were in the room, what Gregor had eaten, how he had conducted himself this time and whether there was not perhaps some slight improvement in his condition. His mother, moreover, began relatively soon to want to visit him, but his father and sister dissuaded her at first with arguments which Gregor listened to very attentively and altogether approved. Later, however, she had to be held back by

zurückhalten, und wenn sie dann rief: "Lasst mich doch
zu Gregor, er ist ja mein unglücklicher Sohn! Begreift ihr
es denn nicht, dass ich zu ihm muss?", dann dachte Gregor,
dass es vielleicht doch gut wäre, wenn die Mutter herein-
käme, nicht jeden Tag natürlich, aber vielleicht einmal in
der Woche; sie verstand doch alles viel besser als die
Schwester, die trotz all ihrem Mute doch nur ein Kind
war und im letzten Grunde vielleicht nur aus kindlichem
Leichtsinn eine so schwere Aufgabe übernommen hatte.

Der Wunsch Gregors, die Mutter zu sehen, ging bald in
Erfüllung. Während des Tages wollte Gregor schon aus
Rücksicht auf seine Eltern sich nicht beim Fenster zeigen,
kriechen konnte er aber auf den paar Quadratmetern des
Fussbodens auch nicht viel, das ruhige Liegen ertrug er
schon während der Nacht schwer, das Essen machte ihm
bald nicht mehr das geringste Vergnügen, und so nahm er
zur Zerstreuung die Gewohnheit an, kreuz und quer über
Wände und Plafond zu kriechen. Besonders oben auf der
Decke hing er gern; es war ganz anders, als das Liegen auf
dem Fussboden; man atmete freier; ein leichtes Schwingen
ging durch den Körper; und in der fast glücklichen Zerstreutheit, in der sich Gregor dort oben befand, konnte es
geschehen, dass er zu seiner eigenen Überraschung sich
losliess und auf den Boden klatschte. Aber nun hatte er
natürlich seinen Körper ganz anders in der Gewalt als
früher und beschädigte sich selbst bei so einem grossen
Falle nicht. Die Schwester nun bemerkte sofort die neue
Unterhaltung, die Gregor für sich gefunden hatte — er
hinterliess ja auch beim Kriechen hie und da Spuren seines
Klebstoffes —, und da setzte sie es sich in den Kopf, Gregor
das Kriechen in grösstem Ausmasse zu ermöglichen und
die Möbel, die es verhinderten, also vor allem den Kasten
und den Schreibtisch, wegzuschaffen. Nun war sie aber nicht
imstande, dies allein zu tun; den Vater wagte sie nicht um
Hilfe zu bitten; das Dienstmädchen hätte ihr ganz gewiss
nicht geholfen, denn dieses etwa sechzehnjährige Mädchen
harrte zwar tapfer seit Entlassung der früheren Köchin

main force, and when she cried out: "Do let me in to Gregor, he is my unfortunate son! Can't you understand that I must go to him?" Gregor thought that it might be well to have her come in, not every day, of course, but perhaps once a week; she understood things, after all, much better than his sister, who was only a child despite the efforts she was making and had perhaps taken on so difficult a task merely out of childish thoughtlessness.

Gregor's desire to see his mother was soon fulfilled. During the daytime he did not want to show himself at the window, out of consideration for his parents, but he could not crawl very far around the few square yards of floor space he had, nor could he bear lying quietly at rest all during the night, while he was fast losing any interest he had ever taken in food, so that for mere recreation he had formed the habit of crawling crisscross over the walls and ceiling. He especially enjoyed hanging suspended from the ceiling; it was much better than lying on the floor; one could breathe more freely; one's body swung and rocked lightly; and in the almost blissful absorption induced by this suspension it could happen to his own surprise that he let go and fell plump on the floor. Yet he now had his body much better under control than formerly, and even such a big fall did him no harm. His sister at once remarked the new distraction Gregor had found for himself—he left traces behind him of the sticky stuff on his soles wherever he crawled—and she got the idea in her head of giving him as wide a field as possible to crawl in and of removing the pieces of furniture that hindered him, above all the chest of drawers and the writing desk. But that was more than she could manage all by herself; she did not dare ask her father to help her; and as for the servant girl, a young creature of sixteen who had had the courage to stay on after the cook's departure, she could not be asked to help, for she had begged

aus, hatte aber um die Vergünstigung gebeten, die Küche unaufhörlich versperrt halten zu dürfen und nur auf besonderen Anruf öffnen zu müssen; so blieb der Schwester also nichts übrig, als einmal in Abwesenheit des Vaters die Mutter zu holen. Mit Ausrufen erregter Freude kam die Mutter auch heran, verstummte aber an der Tür vor Gregors Zimmer. Zuerst sah natürlich die Schwester nach, ob alles im Zimmer in Ordnung war; dann erst liess sie die Mutter eintreten. Gregor hatte in grösster Eile das Leintuch noch tiefer und mehr in Falten gezogen, das Ganze sah wirklich nur wie ein zufällig über das Kanapee geworfenes Leintuch aus. Gregor unterliess auch diesmal, unter dem Leintuch zu spionieren; er verzichtete darauf, die Mutter schon diesmal zu sehen, und war nur froh, dass sie nun doch gekommen war. "Komm nur, man sieht ihn nicht", sagte die Schwester, und offenbar führte sie die Mutter an der Hand. Gregor hörte nun, wie die zwei schwachen Frauen den immerhin schweren alten Kasten von seinem Platze rückten, und wie die Schwester immerfort den grössten Teil der Arbeit für sich beanspruchte, ohne auf die Warnungen der Mutter zu hören, welche fürchtete, dass sie sich überanstrengen werde. Es dauerte sehr lange. Wohl nach schon viertelstündiger Arbeit sagte die Mutter, man solle den Kasten doch lieber hier lassen, denn erstens sei er zu schwer, sie würden vor Ankunft des Vaters nicht fertig werden und mit dem Kasten in der Mitte des Zimmers Gregor jeden Weg verrammeln, zweitens aber sei es doch gar nicht sicher, dass Gregor mit der Entfernung der Möbel ein Gefallen geschehe. Ihr scheine das Gegenteil der Fall zu sein; ihr bedrücke der Anblick der leeren Wand geradezu das Herz; und warum solle nicht auch Gregor diese Empfindung haben, da er doch an die Zimmermöbel längst gewöhnt sei und sich deshalb im leeren Zimmer verlassen fühlen werde. "Und ist es dann nicht so," schloss die Mutter ganz leise, wie sie überhaupt fast flüsterte, als wolle sie vermeiden, dass Gregor, dessen genauen Aufenthalt sie ja nicht kannte, auch nur den Klang der Stimme höre,

as a special favor that she might keep the kitchen door locked and open it only on a definite summons; so there was nothing left but to apply to her mother at an hour when her father was out. And the old lady did come, with exclamations of joyful eagerness, which, however, died away at the door of Gregor's room. Gregor's sister, of course, went in first, to see that everything was in order before letting his mother enter. In great haste Gregor pulled the sheet lower and rucked it more in folds so that it really looked as if it had been thrown accidentally over the sofa. And this time he did not peer out from under it; he renounced the pleasure of seeing his mother on this occasion and was only glad that she had come at all. "Come in, he's out of sight," said his sister, obviously leading her mother in by the hand. Gregor could now hear the two women struggling to shift the heavy old chest from its place, and his sister claiming the greater part of the labor for herself, without listening to the admonitions of her mother who feared she might overstrain herself. It took a long time. After at least a quarter of an hour's tugging his mother objected that the chest had better be left where it was, for in the first place it was too heavy and could never be got out before his father came home, and standing in the middle of the room like that it would only hamper Gregor's movements, while in the second place it was not at all certain that removing the furniture would be doing a service to Gregor. She was inclined to think to the contrary; the sight of the naked walls made her own heart heavy, and why shouldn't Gregor have the same feeling, considering that he had been used to his furniture for so long and might feel forlorn without it. "And doesn't it look," she concluded in a low voice—in fact she had been almost whispering all the time as if to avoid letting Gregor, whose exact whereabouts she did not know, hear even the tones of her voice, for she was convinced that he

denn dass er die Worte nicht verstand, davon war sie
überzeugt, "und ist es nicht so, als ob wir durch die Entfernung der Möbel zeigten, dass wir jede Hoffnung auf
Besserung aufgeben und ihn rücksichtslos sich selbst überlassen? Ich glaube, es wäre das beste, wir suchen das Zimmer genau in dem Zustand zu erhalten, in dem es früher
war, damit Gregor, wenn er wieder zu uns zurückkommt,
alles unverändert findet und um so leichter die Zwischenzeit vergessen kann."

Beim Anhören dieser Worte der Mutter erkannte Gregor, dass der Mangel jeder unmittelbaren menschlichen
Ansprache, verbunden mit dem einförmigen Leben inmitten der Familie, im Laufe dieser zwei Monate seinen
Verstand hatte verwirren müssen, denn anders konnte er es
sich nicht erklären, dass er ernsthaft darnach hatte verlangen können, dass sein Zimmer ausgeleert würde. Hatte er
wirklich Lust, das warme, mit ererbten Möbeln gemütlich
ausgestattete Zimmer in eine Höhle verwandeln zu lassen,
in der er dann freilich nach allen Richtungen ungestört
würde kriechen können, jedoch auch unter gleichzeitigem,
schnellen, gänzlichen Vergessen seiner menschlichen Ver-
gangenheit? War er doch jetzt schon nahe daran, zu
vergessen, und nur die seit langem nicht gehörte Stimme
der Mutter hatte ihn aufgerüttelt. Nichts sollte entfernt
werden; alles musste bleiben; die guten Einwirkungen der
Möbel auf seinen Zustand konnte er nicht entbehren; und
wenn die Möbel ihn hinderten, das sinnlose Herumkriechen
zu betreiben, so war es kein Schaden, sondern ein grosser
Vorteil.

Aber die Schwester war leider anderer Meinung; sie
hatte sich, allerdings nicht ganz unberechtigt, angewöhnt,
bei Besprechung der Angelegenheiten Gregors als besonders Sachverständige gegenüber den Eltern aufzutreten,
und so war auch jetzt der Rat der Mutter für die Schwester
Grund genug, auf der Entfernung nicht nur des Kastens
und des Schreibtisches, an die sie zuerst allein gedacht hatte,
sondern auf der Entfernung sämtlicher Möbel, mit Aus-

could not understand her words—"doesn't it look as if we were showing him, by taking away his furniture, that we have given up hope of his ever getting better and are just leaving him coldly to himself? I think it would be best to keep his room exactly as it has always been, so that when he comes back to us he will find everything unchanged and be able all the more easily to forget what has happened in between."

On hearing these words from his mother Gregor realized that the lack of all direct human speech for the past two months together with the monotony of family life must have confused his mind, otherwise he could not account for the fact that he had quite earnestly looked forward to having his room emptied of furnishing. Did he really want his warm room, so comfortably fitted with old family furniture, to be turned into a naked den in which he would certainly be able to crawl unhampered in all directions but at the price of shedding simultaneously all recollection of his human background? He had indeed been so near the brink of forgetfulness that only the voice of his mother, which he had not heard for so long, had drawn him back from it. Nothing should be taken out of his room; everything must stay as it was; he could not dispense with the good influence of the furniture on his state of mind; and even if the furniture did hamper him in his senseless crawling round and round, that was no drawback but a great advantage.

Unfortunately his sister was of the contrary opinion; she had grown accustomed, and not without reason, to consider herself an expert in Gregor's affairs as against her parents, and so her mother's advice was now enough to make her determined on the removal not only of the chest and the writing desk, which had been her first intention, but of all the furniture except the indispensable sofa. This determination was not, of course, merely

nahme des unentbehrlichen Kanapees, zu bestehen. Es war
natürlich nicht nur kindlicher Trotz und das in der letzten
Zeit so unerwartet und schwer erworbene Selbstvertrauen,
das sie zu dieser Forderung bestimmte; sie hatte doch auch
tatsächlich beobachtet, dass Gregor viel Raum zum Kriechen brauchte, dagegen die Möbel, soweit man sehen
konnte, nicht im geringsten benützte. Vielleicht aber spielte
auch der schwärmerische Sinn der Mädchen ihres Alters
mit, der bei jeder Gelegenheit seine Befriedigung sucht,
und durch den Grete jetzt sich dazu verlocken liess, die
Lage Gregors noch schreckenerregender machen zu wollen,
um dann noch mehr als bis jetzt für ihn leisten zu können.
Denn in einen Raum, in dem Gregor ganz allein die leeren
Wände beherrschte, würde wohl kein Mensch ausser Grete
jemals einzutreten sich getrauen.

Und so liess sie sich von ihrem Entschlusse durch die
Mutter nicht abbringen, die auch in diesem Zimmer vor
lauter Unruhe unsicher schien, bald verstummte und der
Schwester nach Kräften beim Hinausschaffen des Kastens
half. Nun, den Kasten konnte Gregor im Notfall noch entbehren, aber schon der Schreibtisch musste bleiben. Und
kaum hatten die Frauen mit dem Kasten, an den sie sich
ächzend drückten, das Zimmer verlassen, als Gregor den
Kopf unter dem Kanapee hervorstiess, um zu sehen, wie
er vorsichtig und möglichst rücksichtsvoll eingreifen
könnte. Aber zum Unglück war es gerade die Mutter,
welche zuerst zurückkehrte, während Grete im Nebenzimmer den Kasten umfangen hielt und ihn allein hin und
her schwang, ohne ihn natürlich von der Stelle zu bringen.
Die Mutter aber war Gregors Anblick nicht gewöhnt, er
hätte sie krank machen können, und so eilte Gregor er-
schrocken im Rückwärtslauf bis an das andere Ende des
Kanapees, konnte es aber nicht mehr verhindern, dass das
Leintuch vorne ein wenig sich bewegte. Das genügte, um
die Mutter aufmerksam zu machen. Sie stockte, stand einen
Augenblick still und ging dann zu Grete zurück.

Trotzdem sich Gregor immer wieder sagte, dass ja nichts

the outcome of childish recalcitrance and of the self-confidence she had recently developed so unexpectedly and at such cost; she had in fact perceived that Gregor needed a lot of space to crawl about in, while on the other hand he never used the furniture at all, so far as could be seen. Another factor might have been also the enthusiastic temperament of an adolescent girl, which seeks to indulge itself on every opportunity and which now tempted Grete to exaggerate the horror of her brother's circumstances in order that she might do all the more for him. In a room where Gregor lorded it all alone over empty walls no one save herself was likely ever to set foot.

And so she was not to be moved from her resolve by her mother, who seemed moreover to be ill at ease in Gregor's room and therefore unsure of herself, was soon reduced to silence and helped her daughter as best she could to push the chest outside. Now, Gregor could do without the chest, if need be, but the writing desk he must retain. As soon as the two women had got the chest out of his room, groaning as they pushed it, Gregor stuck his head out from under the sofa to see how he might intervene as kindly and cautiously as possible. But as bad luck would have it, his mother was the first to return, leaving Grete clasping the chest in the room next door where she was trying to shift it all by herself, without of course moving it from the spot. His mother however was not accustomed to the sight of him, it might sicken her and so in alarm Gregor backed quickly to the other end of the sofa, yet could not prevent the sheet from swaying a little in front. That was enough to put her on the alert. She paused, stood still for a moment and then went back to Grete.

Although Gregor kept reassuring himself that nothing

Aussergewöhnliches geschehe, sondern nur ein paar Möbel
umgestellt würden, wirkte doch, wie er sich bald einge-
stehen musste, dieses Hin- und Hergehen der Frauen, ihre
kleinen Zurufe, das Kratzen der Möbel auf dem Boden,
wie ein grosser, von allen Seiten genährter Trubel auf ihn,
und er musste sich, so fest er Kopf und Beine an sich zog
und den Leib bis an den Boden drückte, unweigerlich sagen,
dass er das Ganze nicht lange aushalten werde. Sie räumten
ihm sein Zimmer aus; nahmen ihm alles, was ihm lieb
war; den Kasten, in dem die Laubsäge und andere Werk-
zeuge lagen, hatten sie schon hinausgetragen; lockerten
jetzt den schon im Boden fest eingegrabenen Schreibtisch,
an dem er als Handelsakademiker, als Bürgerschüler, ja
sogar schon als Volksschüler seine Aufgaben geschrieben
hatte, — da hatte er wirklich keine Zeit mehr, die guten
Absichten zu prüfen, welche die zwei Frauen hatten, deren
Existenz er übrigens fast vergessen hatte, denn vor Er-
schöpfung arbeiteten sie schon stumm, und man hörte nur
das schwere Tappen ihrer Füsse.

Und so brach er denn hervor — die Frauen stützten sich
gerade im Nebenzimmer an den Schreibtisch, um ein wenig
zu verschnaufen —, wechselte viermal die Richtung des
Laufes, er wusste wirklich nicht, was er zuerst retten sollte,
da sah er an der im übrigen schon leeren Wand auffallend
das Bild der in lauter Pelzwerk gekleideten Dame hängen,
kroch eilends hinauf und presste sich an das Glas, das ihn
festhielt und seinem heissen Bauch wohltat. Dieses Bild
wenigstens, das Gregor jetzt ganz verdeckte, würde nun
gewiss niemand wegnehmen. Er verdrehte den Kopf nach
der Tür des Wohnzimmers, um die Frauen bei ihrer Rück-
kehr zu beobachten.

Sie hatten sich nicht viel Ruhe gegönnt und kamen
schon wieder; Grete hatte den Arm um die Mutter gelegt
und trug sie fast. "Also was nehmen wir jetzt?" sagte

out of the way was happening, but only a few bits of furniture were being changed round, he soon had to admit that all this trotting to and fro of the two women, their little ejaculations and the scraping of furniture along the floor affected him like a vast disturbance coming from all sides at once, and however much he tucked in his head and legs and cowered to the very floor he was bound to confess that he would not be able to stand it for long. They were clearing his room out; taking away everything he loved; the chest in which he kept his fret saw and other tools was already dragged off; they were now loosening the writing desk which had almost sunk into the floor, the desk at which he had done all his homework when he was at the commercial academy, at the grammar school before that, and, yes, even at the primary school—he had no more time to waste in weighing the good intentions of the two women, whose existence he had by now almost forgotten, for they were so exhausted that they were laboring in silence and nothing could be heard but the heavy scuffling of their feet.

And so he rushed out—the women were just leaning against the writing desk in the next room to give themselves a breather—and four times changed his direction, since he really did not know what to rescue first, then on the wall opposite, which was already otherwise cleared, he was struck by the picture of the lady muffled in so much fur and quickly crawled up to it and pressed himself to the glass, which was a good surface to hold on to and comforted his hot belly. This picture at least, which was entirely hidden beneath him, was going to be removed by nobody. He turned his head towards the door of the living room so as to observe the women when they came back.

They had not allowed themselves much of a rest and were already coming; Grete had twined her arm round her mother and was almost supporting her. "Well, what

Grete und sah sich um. Da kreuzten sich ihre Blicke mit
denen Gregors an der Wand. Wohl nur infolge der Gegen-
wart der Mutter behielt sie ihre Fassung, beugte ihr Gesicht zur Mutter, um diese vom Herumschauen abzuhalten,
und sagte, allerdings zitternd und unüberlegt: "Komm,
wollen wir nicht lieber auf einen Augenblick noch ins
Wohnzimmer zurückgehen?" Die Absicht Gretes war für
Gregor klar, sie wollte die Mutter in Sicherheit bringen
und dann ihn von der Wand hinunterjagen. Nun, sie konnte
es ja immerhin versuchen! Er sass auf seinem Bild und gab
es nicht her. Lieber würde er Grete ins Gesicht springen.

Aber Gretes Worte hatten die Mutter erst recht beun-
ruhigt, sie trat zur Seite, erblickte den riesigen braunen
Fleck auf der geblümten Tapete, rief, ehe ihr eigentlich
zum Bewusstsein kam, dass das Gregor war, was sie sah,
mit schreiender, rauher Stimme: "Ach Gott, ach Gott!"
und fiel mit ausgebreiteten Armen, als gebe sie alles auf,
über das Kanapee hin und rührte sich nicht. "Du, Gregor!"
rief die Schwester mit erhobener Faust und eindringlichen
Blicken. Es waren seit der Verwandlung die ersten Worte,
die sie unmittelbar an ihn gerichtet hatte. Sie lief ins Nebenzimmer, um irgendeine Essenz zu holen, mit der sie die
Mutter aus ihrer Ohnmacht wecken könnte; Gregor wollte
auch helfen — zur Rettung des Bildes war noch Zeit —;
er klebte aber fest an dem Glas und musste sich mit Gewalt losreissen; er lief dann auch ins Nebenzimmer, als
könne er der Schwester irgendeinen Rat geben, wie in
früherer Zeit; musste dann aber untätig hinter ihr stehen;
während sie in verschiedenen Fläschchen kramte, erschreckte sie noch, als sie sich umdrehte; eine Flasche fiel
auf den Boden und zerbrach; ein Splitter verletzte Gregor
im Gesicht, irgendeine ätzende Medizin umfloss ihn; Grete
nahm nun, ohne sich länger aufzuhalten, soviel Fläschchen, als sie nur halten konnte, und rannte mit ihnen zur
Mutter hinein; die Tür schlug sie mit dem Fusse zu. Gregor
war nun von der Mutter abgeschlossen, die durch seine
Schuld vielleicht dem Tode nahe war; die Tür durfte er

shall we take now?" said Grete, looking round. Her
eyes met Gregor's from the wall. She kept her composure, presumably because of her mother, bent her
head down to her mother, to keep her from looking up,
and said, although in a fluttering, unpremeditated voice:
"Come, hadn't we better go back to the living room
for a moment?" Her intentions were clear enough to
Gregor, she wanted to bestow her mother in safety and
then chase him down from the wall. Well, just let her
try it! He clung to his picture and would not give it
up. He would rather fly in Grete's face.

But Grete's words had succeeded in disquieting her
mother, who took a step to one side, caught sight of
the huge brown mass on the flowered wallpaper, and
before she was really conscious that what she saw was
Gregor screamed in a loud, hoarse voice: "Oh God, oh
God!" fell with outspread arms over the sofa as if
giving up and did not move. "Gregor!" cried his sister,
shaking her fist and glaring at him. This was the first
time she had directly addressed him since his meta-
morphosis. She ran into the next room for some aro-
matic essence with which to rouse her mother from her
fainting fit. Gregor wanted to help too—there was still
time to rescue the picture—but he was stuck fast to the
glass and had to tear himself loose; he then ran after
his sister into the next room as if he could advise her,
as he used to do; but then had to stand helplessly behind her; she meanwhile searched among various small
bottles and when she turned round started in alarm at
the sight of him; one bottle fell on the floor and broke;
a splinter of glass cut Gregor's face and some kind of
corrosive medicine splashed him; without pausing a
moment longer Grete gathered up all the bottles she
could carry and ran to her mother with them; she
banged the door shut with her foot. Gregor was now
cut off from his mother, who was perhaps nearly dying
because of him; he dared not open the door for fear of

nicht öffnen, wollte er die Schwester, die bei der Mutter bleiben musste, nicht verjagen; er hatte jetzt nichts zu tun, als zu warten; und von Selbstvorwürfen und Besorgnis bedrängt, begann er zu kriechen, überkroch alles, Wände, Möbel und Zimmerdecke und fiel endlich in seiner Verzweiflung, als sich das ganze Zimmer schon um ihn zu drehen anfing, mitten auf den grossen Tisch.

Es verging eine kleine Weile, Gregor lag matt da, ringsherum war es still, vielleicht war das ein gutes Zeichen. Da läutete es. Das Mädchen war natürlich in ihrer Küche eingesperrt und Grete musste daher öffnen gehen. Der Vater war gekommen. "Was ist geschehen?" waren seine ersten Worte; Gretes Aussehen hatte ihm wohl alles verraten. Grete antwortete mit dumpfer Stimme, offenbar drückte sie ihr Gesicht an des Vaters Brust: "Die Mutter war ohnmächtig, aber es geht ihr schon besser. Gregor ist ausgebrochen." "Ich habe es ja erwartet," sagte der Vater, "ich habe es euch ja immer gesagt, aber ihr Frauen wollt nicht hören." Gregor war es klar, dass der Vater Gretes allzukurze Mitteilung schlecht gedeutet hatte und annahm, dass Gregor sich irgendeine Gewalttat habe zuschulden kommen lassen. Deshalb musste Gregor den Vater jetzt zu besänftigen suchen, denn ihn aufzuklären hatte er weder Zeit noch Möglichkeit. Und so flüchtete er sich zur Tür seines Zimmers und drückte sich an sie, damit der Vater beim Eintritt vom Vorzimmer her gleich sehen könne, dass Gregor die beste Absicht habe, sofort in sein Zimmer zurückzukehren, und dass es nicht nötig sei, ihn zurückzutreiben, sondern dass man nur die Tür zu öffnen brauchte, und gleich werde er verschwinden.

Aber der Vater war nicht in der Stimmung, solche Feinheiten zu bemerken. "Ah!" rief er gleich beim Eintritt in einem Tone, als sei er gleichzeitig wütend und froh. Gregor zog den Kopf von der Tür zurück und hob ihn gegen den Vater. So hatte er sich den Vater wirklich nicht vorgestellt, wie er jetzt dastand; allerdings hatte er in der letzten Zeit über dem neuartigen Herumkriechen versäumt, sich so wie

frightening away his sister, who had to stay with her mother; there was nothing he could do but wait; and harassed by self-reproach and worry he began now to crawl to and fro, over everything, walls, furniture and ceiling, and finally, in his despair, when the whole room seemed to be reeling round him, fell down on to the middle of the big table.

A little while elapsed, Gregor was still lying there feebly and all around was quiet, perhaps that was a good omen. Then the doorbell rang. The servant girl was of course locked in her kitchen, and Grete would have to open the door. It was his father. "What's been happening?" were his first words; Grete's face must have told him everything. Grete answered in a muffled voice, apparently hiding her head on his breast: "Mother has been fainting, but she's better now. Gregor's broken loose." "Just what I expected," said his father, "just what I've been telling you, but you women would never listen." It was clear to Gregor that his father had taken the worst interpretation of Grete's all too brief statement and was assuming that Gregor had been guilty of some violent act. Therefore Gregor must now try to propitiate his father, since he had neither time nor means for an explanation. And so he fled to the door of his own room and crouched against it, to let his father see as soon as he came in from the hall that his son had the good intention of getting back into his room immediately and that it was not necessary to drive him there, but that if only the door were opened he would disappear at once.

Yet his father was not in the mood to perceive such fine distinctions. "Ah!" he cried as soon as he appeared, in a tone which sounded at once angry and exultant. Gregor drew his head back from the door and lifted it to look at his father. Truly, this was not the father he had imagined to himself; admittedly he had been too absorbed of late in his new recreation of crawling over

früher um die Vorgänge in der übrigen Wohnung zu
kümmern, und hätte eigentlich darauf gefasst sein müssen,
veränderte Verhältnisse anzutreffen. Trotzdem, trotzdem,
war das noch der Vater? Der gleiche Mann, der müde im
Bett vergraben lag, wenn früher Gregor zu einer Geschäfts-
reise ausgerückt war; der ihn an Abenden der Heimkehr
im Schlafrock im Lehnstuhl empfangen hatte; gar nicht
recht imstande war, aufzustehen, sondern zum Zeichen der
Freude nur die Arme gehoben hatte, und der bei den
seltenen gemeinsamen Spaziergängen an ein paar Sonntagen
im Jahr und an den höchsten Feiertagen zwischen Gregor
und der Mutter, die schon an und für sich langsam gingen,
immer noch ein wenig langsamer, in seinen alten Mantel
eingepackt, mit stets vorsichtig aufgesetztem Krückstock
sich vorwärts arbeitete und, wenn er etwas sagen wollte,
fast immer stillstand und seine Begleitung um sich ver-
sammelte? Nun aber war er recht gut aufgerichtet; in eine
straffe blaue Uniform mit Goldknöpfen gekleidet, wie sie
Diener der Bankinstitute tragen; über dem hohen steifen
Kragen des Rockes entwickelte sich sein starkes Doppel-
kinn; unter den buschigen Augenbrauen drang der Blick
der schwarzen Augen frisch und aufmerksam hervor; das
sonst zerzauste weisse Haar war zu einer peinlich genauen,
leuchtenden Scheitelfrisur niedergekämmt. Er warf seine
Mütze, auf der ein Goldmonogramm, wahrscheinlich das
einer Bank, angebracht war, über das ganze Zimmer im
Bogen auf das Kanapee hin und ging, die Enden seines
langen Uniformrockes zurückgeschlagen, die Hände in den
Hosentaschen, mit verbissenem Gesicht auf Gregor zu. Er
wusste wohl selbst nicht, was er vorhatte; immerhin hob er
die Füsse ungewöhnlich hoch, und Gregor staunte über
die Riesengrösse seiner Stiefelsohlen. Doch hielt er sich
dabei nicht auf, er wusste ja noch vom ersten Tage seines
neuen Lebens her, dass der Vater ihm gegenüber nur die
grösste Strenge für angebracht ansah. Und so lief er vor
dem Vater her, stockte, wenn der Vater stehen blieb, und
eilte schon wieder vorwärts, wenn sich der Vater nur

the ceiling to take the same interest as before in what was happening elsewhere in the flat, and he ought really to be prepared for some changes. And yet, and yet, could that be his father? The man who used to lie wearily sunk in bed whenever Gregor set out on a business journey; who welcomed him back of an evening lying in a long chair in a dressing gown; who could not really rise to his feet but only lifted his arms in greeting, and on the rare occasions when he did go out with his family, on one or two Sundays a year and on high holidays, walked between Gregor and his mother, who were slow walkers anyhow, even more slowly than they did, muffled in his old greatcoat, shuffling laboriously forward with the help of his crook-handled stick which he set down most cautiously at every step and, whenever he wanted to say anything, nearly always came to a full stop and gathered his escort around him? Now he was standing there in fine shape; dressed in a smart blue uniform with gold buttons, such as bank messengers wear; his strong double chin bulged over the stiff high collar of his jacket; from under his bushy eyebrows his black eyes darted fresh and penetrating glances; his onetime tangled white hair had been combed flat on either side of a shining and carefully exact parting. He pitched his cap, which bore a gold monogram, probably the badge of some bank, in a wide sweep across the whole room on to a sofa and with the tail-ends of his jacket thrown back, his hands in his trouser pockets, advanced with a grim visage towards Gregor. Likely enough he did not himself know what he meant to do; at any rate he lifted his feet uncommonly high, and Gregor was dumbfounded at the enormous size of his shoe soles. But Gregor could not risk standing up to him, aware as he had been from the very first day of his new life that his father believed only the severest measures suitable for dealing with him. And so he ran before his father, stopping when he stopped and scut-

rührte. So machten sie mehrmals die Runde um das Zimmer,
ohne dass sich etwas Entscheidendes ereignete, ja ohne dass
das Ganze infolge seines langsamen Tempos den Anschein
einer Verfolgung gehabt hätte. Deshalb blieb auch Gregor
vorläufig auf dem Fussboden, zumal er fürchtete, der Vater
könnte eine Flucht auf die Wände oder den Plafond für
besondere Bosheit halten. Allerdings musste sich Gregor
sagen, dass er sogar dieses Laufen nicht lange aushalten
würde, denn während der Vater einen Schritt machte,
musste er eine Unzahl von Bewegungen ausführen. Atem-
not begann sich schon bemerkbar zu machen, wie er ja
auch in seiner früheren Zeit keine ganz vertrauenswürdige
Lunge besessen hatte. Als er nun so dahintorkelte, um alle
Kräfte für den Lauf zu sammeln, kaum die Augen offen-
hielt; in seiner Stumpfheit an eine andere Rettung als durch
Laufen gar nicht dachte; und fast schon vergessen hatte,
dass ihm die Wände freistanden, die hier allerdings mit
sorgfältig geschnitzten Möbeln voll Zacken und Spitzen
verstellt waren — da flog knapp neben ihm, leicht geschleu-
dert, irgendetwas nieder und rollte vor ihm her. Es war
ein Apfel; gleich flog ihm ein zweiter nach; Gregor blieb
vor Schrecken stehen; ein Weiterlaufen war nutzlos, denn
der Vater hatte sich entschlossen, ihn zu bombardieren.
Aus der Obstschale auf der Kredenz hatte er sich die
Taschen gefüllt und warf nun, ohne vorläufig scharf zu
zielen, Apfel für Apfel. Diese kleinen roten Äpfel rollten
wie elektrisiert auf dem Boden herum und stiessen aneinander. Ein schwach geworfener Apfel streifte Gregors
Rücken, glitt aber unschädlich ab. Ein ihm sofort nachflie-
gender drang dagegen förmlich in Gregors Rücken ein;
Gregor wollte sich weiterschleppen, als könne der überraschende unglaubliche Schmerz mit dem Ortswechsel vergehen; doch fühlte er sich wie festgenagelt und streckte
sich in vollständiger Verwirrung aller Sinne. Nur mit dem
letzten Blick sah er noch, wie die Tür seines Zimmers
aufgerissen wurde, und vor der schreienden Schwester die
Mutter hervoreilte, im Hemd, denn die Schwester hatte sie

tling forward again when his father made any kind of move. In this way they circled the room several times without anything decisive happening, indeed the whole operation did not even look like a pursuit because it was carried out so slowly. And so Gregor did not leave the floor, for he feared that his father might take as a piece of peculiar wickedness any excursion of his over the walls or the ceiling. All the same, he could not stay this course much longer, for while his father took one step he had to carry out a whole series of movements. He was already beginning to feel breathless, just as in his former life his lungs had not been very dependable. As he was staggering along, trying to concentrate his energy on running, hardly keeping his eyes open; in his dazed state never even thinking of any other escape than simply going forward; and having almost forgotten that the walls were free to him, which in this room were well provided with finely carved pieces of furniture full of knobs and crevices—suddenly something lightly flung landed close behind him and rolled before him. It was an apple; a second apple followed immediately; Gregor came to a stop in alarm; there was no point in running on, for his father was determined to bombard him. He had filled his pockets with fruit from the dish on the sideboard and was now shying apple after apple, without taking particularly good aim for the moment. The small red apples rolled about the floor as if magnetized and cannoned into each other. An apple thrown without much force grazed Gregor's back and glanced off harmlessly. But another following immediately landed right on his back and sank in; Gregor wanted to drag himself forward, as if this startling, incredible pain could be left behind him; but he felt as if nailed to the spot and flattened himself out in a complete derangement of all his senses. With his last conscious look he saw the door of his room being torn open and his mother rushing out ahead of his

entkleidet, um ihr in der Ohnmacht Atemfreiheit zu verschaffen, wie dann die Mutter auf den Vater zulief und ihr auf dem Weg die aufgebundenen Röcke einer nach dem anderen zu Boden glitten, und wie sie stolpernd über die Röcke auf den Vater eindrang und ihn umarmend, in gänzlicher Vereinigung mit ihm — nun versagte aber Gregors Sehkraft schon — die Hände an des Vaters Hinterkopf um Schonung von Gregors Leben bat.

III

DIE SCHWERE Verwundung Gregors, an der er über einen Monat litt — der Apfel blieb, da ihn niemand zu entfernen wagte, als sichtbares Andenken im Fleische sitzen —, schien selbst den Vater daran erinnert zu haben, dass Gregor trotz seiner gegenwärtigen traurigen und ekelhaften Gestalt ein Familienmitglied war, das man nicht wie einen Feind behandeln durfte, sondern dem gegenüber es das Gebot der Familienpflicht war, den Widerwillen hinunterzuschlucken und zu dulden, nichts als zu dulden.

Und wenn nun auch Gregor durch seine Wunde an Beweglichkeit wahrscheinlich für immer verloren hatte und vorläufig zur Durchquerung seines Zimmers wie ein alter Invalide lange, lange Minuten brauchte — an das Kriechen in der Höhe war nicht zu denken —, so bekam er für diese Verschlimmerung seines Zustandes einen seiner Meinung nach vollständig genügenden Ersatz dadurch, dass immer gegen Abend die Wohnzimmertür, die er schon ein bis zwei Stunden vorher scharf zu beobachten pflegte, geöffnet wurde, so dass er, im Dunkel seines Zimmers liegend, vom Wohnzimmer aus unsichtbar, die ganze Familie beim beleuchteten Tische sehen und ihre Reden, gewissermassen mit allgemeiner Erlaubnis, also ganz anders als früher, anhören durfte.

screaming sister, in her underbodice, for her daughter
had loosened her clothing to let her breathe more freely
and recover from her swoon, he saw his mother rushing
towards his father, leaving one after another behind
her on the floor her loosened petticoats, stumbling over
her petticoats straight to his father and embracing him,
in complete union with him—but here Gregor's sight
began to fail—with her hands clasped round his father's
neck as she begged for her son's life.

III

THE SERIOUS INJURY done to Gregor, which disabled
him for more than a month—the apple went on sticking
in his body as a visible reminder, since no one ventured to remove it—seemed to have made even his
father recollect that Gregor was a member of the
family, despite his present unfortunate and repulsive
shape, and ought not to be treated as an enemy, that, on
the contrary, family duty required the suppression of
disgust and the exercise of patience, nothing but
patience.

And although his injury had impaired, probably for
ever, his powers of movement, and for the time being
it took him long, long minutes to creep across his room
like an old invalid—there was no question now of
crawling up the wall—yet in his own opinion he was
sufficiently compensated for this worsening of his condition by the fact that towards evening the living-room
door, which he used to watch intently for an hour or
two beforehand, was always thrown open, so that lying
in the darkness of his room, invisible to the family, he
could see them all at the lamp-lit table and listen to their
talk, by general consent as it were, very different from
his earlier eavesdropping.

Freilich waren es nicht mehr die lebhaften Unterhaltungen der früheren Zeiten, an die Gregor in den kleinen Hotelzimmern stets mit einigem Verlangen gedacht hatte, wenn er sich müde in das feuchte Bettzeug hatte werfen müssen. Es ging jetzt meist nur sehr still zu. Der Vater schlief bald nach dem Nachtessen in seinem Sessel ein; die Mutter und Schwester ermahnten einander zur Stille; die Mutter nähte, weit unter das Licht vorgebeugt, feine Wäsche für ein Modengeschäft; die Schwester, die eine Stellung als Verkäuferin angenommen hatte, lernte am Abend Stenographie und Französisch, um vielleicht später einmal einen besseren Posten zu erreichen. Manchmal wachte der Vater auf, und als wisse er gar nicht, dass er geschlafen habe, sagte er zur Mutter: "Wie lange du heute schon wieder nähst!" und schlief sofort wieder ein, während Mutter und Schwester einander müde zulächelten.

Mit einer Art Eigensinn weigerte sich der Vater, auch zu Hause seine Dieneruniform abzulegen; und während der Schlafrock nutzlos am Kleiderhaken hing, schlummerte der Vater vollständig angezogen auf seinem Platz, als sei er immer zu seinem Dienste bereit und warte auch hier auf die Stimme des Vorgesetzten. Infolgedessen verlor die gleich anfangs nicht neue Uniform trotz aller Sorgfalt von Mutter und Schwester an Reinlichkeit, und Gregor sah oft ganze Abende lang auf dieses über und über fleckige, mit seinen stets geputzten Goldknöpfen leuchtende Kleid, in dem der alte Mann höchst unbequem und doch ruhig schlief.

Sobald die Uhr zehn schlug, suchte die Mutter durch leise Zusprache den Vater zu wecken und dann zu überreden, ins Bett zu gehen, denn hier war es doch kein richtiger Schlaf und diesen hatte der Vater, der um sechs Uhr seinen Dienst antreten musste, äusserst nötig. Aber in dem Eigensinn, der ihn, seitdem er Diener war, ergriffen hatte, bestand er immer darauf, noch länger bei Tisch zu bleiben, trotzdem er regelmässig einschlief, und war dann

True, their intercourse lacked the lively character of former times, which he had always called to mind with a certain wistfulness in the small hotel bedrooms where he had been wont to throw himself down, tired out, on damp bedding. They were now mostly very silent. Soon after supper his father would fall asleep in his armchair; his mother and sister would admonish each other to be silent; his mother, bending low over the lamp, stitched at fine sewing for an underwear firm; his sister, who had taken a job as a salesgirl, was learning shorthand and French in the evenings on the chance of bettering herself. Sometimes his father woke up, and as if quite unaware that he had been sleeping said to his mother: "What a lot of sewing you're doing today!" and at once fell asleep again, while the two women exchanged a tired smile.

With a kind of mulishness his father persisted in keeping his uniform on even in the house; his dressing gown hung uselessly on its peg and he slept fully dressed where he sat, as if he were ready for service at any moment and even here only at the beck and call of his superior. As a result, his uniform, which was not brand-new to start with, began to look dirty, despite all the loving care of the mother and sister to keep it clean, and Gregor often spent whole evenings gazing at the many greasy spots on the garment, gleaming with gold buttons always in a high state of polish, in which the old man sat sleeping in extreme discomfort and yet quite peacefully.

As soon as the clock struck ten his mother tried to rouse his father with gentle words and to persuade him after that to get into bed, for sitting there he could not have a proper sleep and that was what he needed most, since he had to go on duty at six. But with the mulishness that had obsessed him since he became a bank messenger he always insisted on staying longer at the table, although he regularly fell asleep again and

überdies nur mit der grössten Mühe zu bewegen, den Sessel mit dem Bett zu vertauschen. Da mochten Mutter und Schwester mit kleinen Ermahnungen noch so sehr auf ihn eindringen, viertelstundenlang schüttelte er langsam den Kopf, hielt die Augen geschlossen und stand nicht auf. Die Mutter zupfte ihn am Ärmel, sagte ihm Schmeichelworte ins Ohr, die Schwester verliess ihre Aufgabe, um der Mutter zu helfen, aber beim Vater verfing das nicht. Er versank nur noch tiefer in seinen Sessel. Erst bis ihn die Frauen unter den Achseln fassten, schlug er die Augen auf, sah abwechselnd die Mutter und die Schwester an und pflegte zu sagen: "Das ist ein Leben. Das ist die Ruhe meiner alten Tage." Und auf die beiden Frauen gestützt, erhob er sich, umständlich, als sei er für sich selbst die grösste Last, liess sich von den Frauen bis zur Türe führen, winkte ihnen dort ab und ging nun selbständig weiter, während die Mutter ihr Nähzeug, die Schwester ihre Feder eiligst hinwarfen, um hinter dem Vater zu laufen und ihm weiter behilflich zu sein.

Wer hatte in dieser abgearbeiteten und übermüdeten Familie Zeit, sich um Gregor mehr zu kümmern, als unbedingt nötig war? Der Haushalt wurde immer mehr eingeschränkt; das Dienstmädchen wurde nun doch entlassen; eine riesige knochige Bedienerin mit weissem, den Kopf umflatterndem Haar kam des Morgens und des Abends, um die schwerste Arbeit zu leisten; alles andere besorgte die Mutter neben ihrer vielen Näharbeit. Es geschah sogar, dass verschiedene Familienschmuckstücke, welche früher die Mutter und die Schwester überglücklich bei Unterhaltungen und Feierlichkeiten getragen hatten, verkauft wurden, wie Gregor am Abend aus der allgemeinen Besprechung der erzielten Preise erfuhr. Die grösste Klage war aber stets, dass man diese für die gegenwärtigen Verhältnisse allzugrosse Wohnung nicht verlassen konnte, da es nicht auszudenken war, wie man Gregor übersiedeln sollte. Aber Gregor sah wohl ein, dass es nicht nur die Rücksicht auf

in the end only with the greatest trouble could be got out of his armchair and into his bed. However insistently Gregor's mother and sister kept urging him with gentle reminders, he would go on slowly shaking his head for a quarter of an hour, keeping his eyes shut, and refuse to get to his feet. The mother plucked at his sleeve, whispering endearments in his ear, the sister left her lessons to come to her mother's help, but it had no effect on Gregor's father. He would only sink down deeper in his chair. Not until the two women hoisted him up by the armpits did he open his eyes and look at them both, one after the other, usually with the remark: "This is a life. This is the peace and quiet of my old age." And leaning on the two of them he would heave himself up, with difficulty, as if he were a great burden to himself, suffer them to lead him as far as the door and then wave them off and go on alone, while the mother abandoned her needlework and the sister her pen in order to run after him and help him further.

Who could find time, in this overworked and tired-out family, to bother about Gregor more than was absolutely needful? The household was reduced more and more; the servant girl was turned off; a gigantic bony charwoman with white hair flying round her head came in morning and evening to do the rough work; everything else was done by Gregor's mother, as well as great piles of sewing. Even various family ornaments, which his mother and sister used to wear with pride at parties and celebrations, had to be sold, as Gregor discovered of an evening from hearing them all discuss the prices obtained. But what they lamented most was the fact that they could not leave the flat which was much too big for their present circumstances, because they could not think of any way to shift Gregor. Yet Gregor saw well enough that consideration for him was not the main difficulty preventing the removal, for

ihn war, welche eine Übersiedlung verhinderte, denn ihn
hätte man doch in einer passenden Kiste mit ein paar Luft-
löchern leicht transportieren können; was die Familie haupt-
sächlich vom Wohnungswechsel abhielt, war vielmehr die
völlige Hoffnungslosigkeit und der Gedanke daran, dass
sie mit einem Unglück geschlagen war, wie niemand sonst
im ganzen Verwandten- und Bekanntenkreis. Was die Welt
von armen Leuten verlangt, erfüllten sie bis zum äussersten,
der Vater holte den kleinen Bankbeamten das Frühstück,
die Mutter opferte sich für die Wäsche fremder Leute,
die Schwester lief nach dem Befehl der Kunden hinter dem
Pulte hin und her, aber weiter reichten die Kräfte der
Familie schon nicht. Und die Wunde im Rücken fing Gregor wie neu zu schmerzen an, wenn Mutter und Schwester,
nachdem sie den Vater zu Bett gebracht hatten, nun zu-
rückkehrten, die Arbeit liegen liessen, nahe zusammen-
rückten, schon Wange an Wange sassen; wenn jetzt die
Mutter, auf Gregors Zimmer zeigend, sagte: "Mach' dort
die Tür zu, Grete", und wenn nun Gregor wieder im
Dunkel war, während nebenan die Frauen ihre Tränen
vermischten oder gar tränenlos den Tisch anstarrten.

Die Nächte und Tage verbrachte Gregor fast ganz ohne
Schlaf. Manchmal dachte er daran, beim nächsten Öffnen
der Tür die Angelegenheiten der Familie ganz so wie früher
wieder in die Hand zu nehmen; in seinen Gedanken erschienen wieder nach langer Zeit der Chef und der Prokurist, die Kommis und die Lehrjungen, der so begriffstützige
Hausknecht, zwei drei Freunde aus anderen Geschäften,
ein Stubenmädchen aus einem Hotel in der Provinz, eine
liebe, flüchtige Erinnerung, eine Kassiererin aus einem Hut-
geschäft, um die er sich ernsthaft, aber zu langsam bewor-
ben hatte — sie alle erschienen untermischt mit Fremden
oder schon Vergessenen, aber statt ihm und seiner Familie
zu helfen, waren ·sie sämtlich unzugänglich, und er war
froh, wenn sie verschwanden. Dann aber war er wieder
gar nicht in der Laune, sich um seine Familie zu sorgen,
bloss Wut über die schlechte Wartung erfüllte ihn, und

they could have easily shifted him in some suitable
box with a few air holes in it; what really kept them
from moving into another flat was rather their own
complete hopelessness and the belief that they had been
singled out for a misfortune such as had never happened to any of their relations or acquaintances. They
fulfilled to the utmost all that the world demands of
poor people, the father fetched breakfast for the small
clerks in the bank, the mother devoted her energy to
making underwear for strangers, the sister trotted to
and fro behind the counter at the behest of customers,
but more than this they had not the strength to do.
And the wound in Gregor's back began to nag at him
afresh when his mother and sister, after getting his
father into bed, came back again, left their work lying,
drew close to each other and sat cheek by cheek;
when his mother, pointing towards his room, said: "Shut
that door now, Grete," and he was left again in darkness, while next door the women mingled their tears or
perhaps sat dry-eyed staring at the table.

Gregor hardly slept at all by night or by day. He
was often haunted by the idea that next time the door
opened he would take the family's affairs in hand again
just as he used to do; once more, after this long inter-
val, there appeared in his thoughts the figures of the
chief and the chief clerk, the commercial travelers and
the apprentices, the porter who was so dull-witted, two
or three friends in other firms, a chambermaid in one
of the rural hotels, a sweet and fleeting memory, a
cashier in a milliner's shop, whom he had wooed earnestly but too slowly—they all appeared, together with
strangers or people he had quite forgotten, but instead
of helping him and his family they were one and all
unapproachable and he was glad when they vanished.
At other times he would not be in the mood to bother
about his family, he was only filled with rage at the way

trotzdem er sich nichts vorstellen konnte, worauf er Appe-
tit gehabt hätte, machte er doch Pläne, wie er in die Speise-
kammer gelangen könnte, um dort zu nehmen, was ihm,
auch wenn er keinen Hunger hatte, immerhin gebührte.
Ohne jetzt mehr nachzudenken, womit man Gregor einen
besonderen Gefallen machen könnte, schob die Schwester
eiligst, ehe sie morgens und mittags ins Geschäft lief, mit
dem Fuss irgendeine beliebige Speise in Gregors Zimmer
hinein, um sie am Abend, gleichgültig dagegen, ob die
Speise vielleicht nur gekostet oder — der häufigste Fall —
gänzlich unberührt war, mit einem Schwenken des Besens
hinauszukehren. Das Aufräumen des Zimmers, das sie nun
immer abends besorgte, konnte gar nicht mehr schneller
getan sein. Schmutzstreifen zogen sich die Wände entlang,
hie und da lagen Knäuel von Staub und Unrat. In der ersten
Zeit stellte sich Gregor bei der Ankunft der Schwester in
derartige besonders bezeichnende Winkel, um ihr durch
diese Stellung gewissermassen einen Vorwurf zu machen.
Aber er hätte wohl wochenlang dort bleiben können, ohne
dass sich die Schwester gebessert hätte; sie sah ja den
Schmutz genau so wie er, aber sie hatte sich eben entschlossen, ihn zu lassen. Dabei wachte sie mit einer an ihr
ganz neuen Empfindlichkeit, die überhaupt die ganze Familie ergriffen hatte, darüber, dass das Aufräumen von
Gregors Zimmer ihr vorbehalten blieb. Einmal hatte die
Mutter Gregors Zimmer einer grossen Reinigung unter-
zogen, die ihr nur nach Verbrauch einiger Kübel Wasser
gelungen war — die viele Feuchtigkeit kränkte allerdings
Gregor auch und er lag breit, verbittert und unbeweglich
auf dem Kanapee —, aber die Strafe blieb für die Mutter
nicht aus. Denn kaum hatte am Abend die Schwester die
Veränderung in Gregors Zimmer bemerkt, als sie, aufs
höchste beleidigt, ins Wohnzimmer lief und, trotz der be-
schwörend erhobenen Hände der Mutter, in einen Wein-
krampf ausbrach, dem die Eltern — der Vater war natürlich
aus seinem Sessel aufgeschreckt worden — zuerst erstaunt
und hilflos zusahen; bis auch sie sich zu rühren anfingen;

they were neglecting him, and although he had no clear idea of what he might care to eat he would make plans for getting into the larder to take the food that was after all his due, even if he were not hungry. His sister no longer took thought to bring him what might especially please him, but in the morning and at noon before she went to business hurriedly pushed into his room with her foot any food that was available, and in the evening cleared it out again with one sweep of the broom, heedless of whether it had been merely tasted, or—as most frequently happened—left untouched. The cleaning of his room, which she now did always in the evenings, could not have been more hastily done. Streaks of dirt stretched along the walls, here and there lay balls of dust and filth. At first Gregor used to station himself in some particularly filthy corner when his sister arrived, in order to reproach her with it, so to speak. But he could have sat there for weeks without getting her to make any improvement; she could see the dirt as well as he did, but she had simply made up her mind to leave it alone. And yet, with a touchiness that was new to her, which seemed anyhow to have infected the whole family, she jealously guarded her claim to be the sole caretaker of Gregor's room. His mother once subjected his room to a thorough cleaning, which was achieved only by means of several buckets of water—all this dampness of course upset Gregor too and he lay widespread, sulky and motionless on the sofa—but she was well punished for it. Hardly had his sister noticed the changed aspect of his room that evening than she rushed in high dudgeon into the living room and, despite the imploringly raised hands of her mother, burst into a storm of weeping, while her parents—her father had of course been startled out of his chair—looked on at first in helpless amazement; then they too began to go into action; the father reproached the mother on his right for not having

der Vater rechts der Mutter Vorwürfe machte, dass sie
Gregors Zimmer nicht der Schwester zur Reinigung über-
liess; links dagegen die Schwester anschrie, sie werde
niemals mehr Gregors Zimmer reinigen dürfen; während
die Mutter den Vater, der sich vor Erregung nicht mehr
kannte, ins Schlafzimmer zu schleppen suchte; die Schwester, von Schluchzen geschüttelt, mit ihren kleinen Fäusten
den Tisch bearbeitete; und Gregor laut vor Wut darüber
zischte, dass es keinem einfiel, die Tür zu schliessen und
ihm diesen Anblick und Lärm zu ersparen.

Aber selbst wenn die Schwester, erschöpft von ihrer
Berufsarbeit, dessen überdrüssig geworden war, für Gregor,
wie früher, zu sorgen, so hätte noch keineswegs die Mutter
für sie eintreten müssen und Gregor hätte doch nicht
vernachlässigt zu werden brauchen. Denn nun war die
Bedienerin da. Diese alte Witwe, die in ihrem langen Leben
mit Hilfe ihres starken Knochenbaues das Ärgste über-
standen haben mochte, hatte keinen eigentlichen Abscheu
vor Gregor. Ohne irgendwie neugierig zu sein, hatte sie
zufällig einmal die Tür von Gregors Zimmer aufgemacht
und war im Anblick Gregors, der, gänzlich überrascht,
trotzdem ihn niemand jagte, hin- und herzulaufen begann,
die Hände im Schoss gefaltet staunend stehen geblieben.
Seitdem versäumte sie nicht, stets flüchtig morgens und
abends die Tür ein wenig zu öffnen und zu Gregor hin-
einzuschauen. Anfangs rief sie ihn auch zu sich herbei,
mit Worten, die sie wahrscheinlich für freundlich hielt, wie
"Komm mal herüber, alter Mistkäfer!" oder "Seht mal den
alten Mistkäfer!" Auf solche Ansprachen antwortete Gregor mit nichts, sondern blieb unbeweglich auf seinem Platz,
als sei die Tür gar nicht geöffnet worden. Hätte man doch
dieser Bedienerin, statt sie nach ihrer Laune ihn nutzlos
stören zu lassen, lieber den Befehl gegeben, sein Zimmer
täglich zu reinigen! Einmal am frühen Morgen — ein hef-
tiger Regen, vielleicht schon ein Zeichen des kommenden
Frühjahrs, schlug an die Scheiben — war Gregor, als die
Bedienerin mit ihren Redensarten wieder begann, derartig

left the cleaning of Gregor's room to his sister; shrieked at the sister on his left that never again was she to be allowed to clean Gregor's room; while the mother tried to pull the father into his bedroom, since he was beyond himself with agitation; the sister, shaken with sobs, then beat upon the table with her small fists; and Gregor hissed loudly with rage because not one of them thought of shutting the door to spare him such a spectacle and so much noise.

Still, even if the sister, exhausted by her daily work, had grown tired of looking after Gregor as she did formerly, there was no need for his mother's intervention or for Gregor's being neglected at all. The charwoman was there. This old widow, whose strong bony frame had enabled her to survive the worst a long life could offer, by no means recoiled from Gregor. Without being in the least curious she had once by chance opened the door of his room and at the sight of Gregor, who, taken by surprise, began to rush to and fro although no one was chasing him, merely stood there with her arms folded. From that time she never failed to open his door a little for a moment, morning and evening, to have a look at him. At first she even used to call him to her, with words which apparently she took to be friendly, such as: "Come along, then, you old dung beetle!" or "Look at the old dung beetle, then!" To such allocutions Gregor made no answer, but stayed motionless where he was, as if the door had never been opened. Instead of being allowed to disturb him so senselessly whenever the whim took her, she should rather have been ordered to clean out his room daily, that charwoman! Once, early in the morning—heavy rain was lashing on the windowpanes, perhaps a sign that spring was on the way—Gregor was so exasperated when she began addressing him again that he ran at her, as if to attack her, although slowly and feebly enough. But the

erbittert, dass er, wie zum Angriff, allerdings langsam und
hinfällig, sich gegen sie wendete. Die Bedienerin aber, statt
sich zu fürchten, hob bloss einen in der Nähe der Tür
befindlichen Stuhl hoch empor, und wie sie mit gross
geöffnetem Munde dastand, war ihre Absicht klar, den
Mund erst zu schliessen, wenn der Sessel in ihrer Hand auf
Gregors Rücken niederschlagen würde. "Also weiter geht
es nicht?" fragte sie, als Gregor sich wieder umdrehte,
und stellte den Sessel ruhig in die Ecke zurück.

Gregor ass nun fast gar nichts mehr. Nur wenn er zufällig an der vorbereiteten Speise vorüberkam, nahm er
zum Spiel einen Bissen in den Mund, hielt ihn dort
stundenlang und spie ihn dann meist wieder aus. Zuerst
dachte er, es sei die Trauer über den Zustand seines Zimmers, die ihn vom Essen abhalte, aber gerade mit den
Veränderungen des Zimmers söhnte er sich sehr bald aus.
Man hatte sich angewöhnt, Dinge, die man anderswo nicht
unterbringen konnte, in dieses Zimmer hineinzustellen, und
solcher Dinge gab es nun viele, da man ein Zimmer der
Wohnung an drei Zimmerherren vermietet hatte. Diese
ernsten Herren — alle drei hatten Vollbärte, wie Gregor
einmal durch eine Türspalte feststellte — waren peinlich
auf Ordnung, nicht nur in ihrem Zimmer, sondern, da sie
sich nun einmal hier eingemietet hatten, in der ganzen
Wirtschaft, also insbesondere in der Küche, bedacht. Un-
nützen oder gar schmutzigen Kram ertrugen sie nicht.
Überdies hatten sie zum grössten Teil ihre eigenen Ein-
richtungsstücke mitgebracht. Aus diesem Grunde waren
viele Dinge überflüssig geworden, die zwar nicht ver-
käuflich waren, die man aber auch nicht wegwerfen wollte.
Alle diese wanderten in Gregors Zimmer. Ebenso auch die
Aschenkiste und die Abfallkiste aus der Küche. Was nur
im Augenblick unbrauchbar war, schleuderte die Bedienerin,
die es immer sehr eilig hatte, einfach in Gregors Zimmer;
Gregor sah glücklicherweise meist nur den betreffenden
Gegenstand und die Hand, die ihn hielt. Die Bedienerin
hatte vielleicht die Absicht, bei Zeit und Gelegenheit die

charwoman instead of showing fright merely lifted high a chair that happened to be beside the door, and as she stood there with her mouth wide open it was clear that she meant to shut it only when she brought the chair down on Gregor's back. "So you're not coming any nearer?" she asked, as Gregor turned away again, and quietly put the chair back into the corner.

Gregor was now eating hardly anything. Only when he happened to pass the food laid out for him did he take a bit of something in his mouth as a pastime, kept it there for an hour at a time and usually spat it out again. At first he thought it was chagrin over the state of his room that prevented him from eating, yet he soon got used to the various changes in his room. It had become a habit in the family to push into his room things there was no room for elsewhere, and there were plenty of these now, since one of the rooms had been let to three lodgers. These serious gentlemen—all three of them with full beards, as Gregor once observed through a crack in the door—had a passion for order, not only in their own room but, since they were now members of the household, in all its arrangements, especially in the kitchen. Superfluous, not to say dirty, objects they could not bear. Besides, they had brought with them most of the furnishings they needed. For this reason many things could be dispensed with that it was no use trying to sell but that should not be thrown away either. All of them found their way into Gregor's room. The ash can likewise and the kitchen garbage can. Anything that was not needed for the moment was simply flung into Gregor's room by the charwoman, who did everything in a hurry; fortunately Gregor usually saw only the object, whatever it was, and the hand that held it. Perhaps she intended to take the things away again as time and opportunity offered, or to collect them until she could throw

Dinge wieder zu holen oder alle insgesamt mit einemmal hinauszuwerfen, tatsächlich aber blieben sie dort liegen, wohin sie durch den ersten Wurf gekommen waren, wenn nicht Gregor sich durch das Rumpelzeug wand und es in Bewegung brachte, zuerst gezwungen, weil kein sonstiger Platz zum Kriechen frei war, später aber mit wachsendem Vergnügen, obwohl er nach solchen Wanderungen, zum Sterben müde und traurig, wieder stundenlang sich nicht rührte.

Da die Zimmerherren manchmal auch ihr Abendessen zu Hause im gemeinsamen Wohnzimmer einnahmen, blieb die Wohnzimmertür an manchen Abenden geschlossen, aber Gregor verzichtete ganz leicht auf das Öffnen der Tür, hatte er doch schon manche Abende, an denen sie geöffnet war, nicht ausgenützt, sondern war, ohne dass es die Familie merkte, im dunkelsten Winkel seines Zimmers gelegen. Einmal aber hatte die Bedienerin die Tür zum Wohnzimmer ein wenig offen gelassen, und sie blieb so offen, auch als die Zimmerherren am Abend eintraten und Licht gemacht wurde. Sie setzten sich oben an den Tisch, wo in früheren Zeiten der Vater, die Mutter und Gregor gegessen hatten, entfalteten die Servietten und nahmen Messer und Gabel in die Hand. Sofort erschien in der Tür die Mutter mit einer Schüssel Fleisch und knapp hinter ihr die Schwester mit einer Schüssel hochgeschichteter Kartoffeln. Das Essen dampfte mit starkem Rauch. Die Zimmerherren beugten sich über die vor sie hingestellten Schüsseln, als wollten sie sie vor dem Essen prüfen, und tatsächlich zerschnitt der, welcher in der Mitte sass und den anderen zwei als Autorität zu gelten schien, ein Stück Fleisch noch auf der Schüssel, offenbar um festzustellen, ob es mürbe genug sei und ob es nicht etwa in die Küche zurückgeschickt werden solle. Er war befriedigt, und Mutter und Schwester, die gespannt zugesehen hatten, begannen aufatmend zu lächeln.

Die Familie selbst ass in der Küche. Trotzdem kam der Vater, ehe er in die Küche ging, in dieses Zimmer herein und machte mit einer einzigen Verbeugung, die Kappe in

them all out in a heap, but in fact they just lay wherever she happened to throw them, except when Gregor pushed his way through the junk heap and shifted it somewhat, at first out of necessity, because he had not room enough to crawl, but later with increasing enjoyment, although after such excursions, being sad and weary to death, he would lie motionless for hours.

Since the lodgers often ate their supper at home in the common living room, the living-room door stayed shut many an evening, yet Gregor reconciled himself quite easily to the shutting of the door, for often enough on evenings when it was opened he had disregarded it entirely and lain in the darkest corner of his room, quite unnoticed by the family. But on one occasion the charwoman left the door open a little and it stayed ajar even when the lodgers came in for supper and the lamp was lit. They set themselves at the top end of the table where formerly Gregor and his father and mother had eaten their meals, unfolded their napkins and took knife and fork in hand. At once his mother appeared in the other doorway with a dish of meat and close behind her his sister with a dish of potatoes piled high. The food steamed with a thick vapor. The lodgers bent over the food set before them as if to scrutinize it before eating, in fact the man in the middle, who seemed to pass for an authority with the other two, cut a piece of meat as it lay on the dish, obviously to discover if it were tender or should be sent back to the kitchen. He showed satisfaction, and Gregor's mother and sister, who had been watching anxiously, breathed freely and began to smile.

The family itself took its meals in the kitchen. None the less, Gregor's father came into the living room before going into the kitchen and with one prolonged bow,

der Hand, einen Rundgang um den Tisch. Die Zimmerherren erhoben sich sämtlich und murmelten etwas in ihre
Bärte. Als sie dann allein waren, assen sie fast unter voll-
kommenem Stillschweigen. Sonderbar schien es Gregor,
dass man aus allen mannigfachen Geräuschen des Essens
immer wieder ihre kauenden Zähne heraushörte, als ob damit
Gregor gezeigt werden sollte, dass man Zähne brauche,
um zu essen, und dass man auch mit den schönsten zahn-
losen Kiefern nichts ausrichten könne. "Ich habe ja Appe-
tit," sagte sich Gregor sorgenvoll, "aber nicht auf diese
Dinge. Wie sich diese Zimmerherren nähren, und ich
komme um!"

Gerade an diesem Abend — Gregor erinnerte sich nicht,
während der ganzen Zeit die Violine gehört zu haben —
ertönte sie von der Küche her. Die Zimmerherren hatten
schon ihr Nachtmahl beendet, der mittlere hatte die Zeitung
hervorgezogen, den zwei anderen je ein Blatt gegeben, und
nun lasen sie zurückgelehnt und rauchten. Als die Violine
zu spielen begann, wurden sie aufmerksam, erhoben sich
und gingen auf den Fusspitzen zur Vorzimmertür, in der
sie aneinandergedrängt stehen blieben. Man musste sie von
der Küche aus gehört haben, denn der Vater rief: "Ist den
Herren das Spiel vielleicht unangenehm? Es kann sofort
eingestellt werden." "Im Gegenteil," sagte der mittlere
der Herren, "möchte das Fräulein nicht zu uns hereinkommen und hier im Zimmer spielen, wo es doch viel be-
quemer und gemütlicher ist?" "O bitte", rief der Vater,
als sei er der Violinspieler. Die Herren traten ins Zimmer
zurück und warteten. Bald kam der Vater mit dem Notenpult, die Mutter mit den Noten und die Schwester mit der
Violine. Die Schwester bereitete alles ruhig zum Spiele vor;
die Eltern, die niemals früher Zimmer vermietet hatten
und deshalb die Höflichkeit gegen die Zimmerherren über-
trieben, wagten gar nicht, sich auf ihre eigenen Sessel zu
setzen; der Vater lehnte an der Tür, die rechte Hand
zwischen zwei Knöpfe des geschlossenen Livreerockes ge-
steckt; die Mutter aber erhielt von einem Herrn einen Sessel

cap in hand, made a round of the table. The lodgers all stood up and murmured something in their beards. When they were alone again they ate their food in almost complete silence. It seemed remarkable to Gregor that among the various noises coming from the table he could always distinguish the sound of their masticating teeth, as if this were a sign to Gregor that one needed teeth in order to eat, and that with toothless jaws even of the finest make one could do nothing. "I'm hungry enough," said Gregor sadly to himself, "but not for that kind of food. How these lodgers are stuffing themselves, and here am I dying of starvation!"

On that very evening—during the whole of his time there Gregor could not remember ever having heard the violin—the sound of violin playing came from the kitchen. The lodgers had already finished their supper, the one in the middle had brought out a newspaper and given the other two a page apiece, and now they were leaning back at ease reading and smoking. When the violin began to play they pricked up their ears, got to their feet, and went on tiptoe to the hall door where they stood huddled together. Their movements must have been heard in the kitchen, for Gregor's father called out: "Is the violin playing disturbing you, gentlemen? It can be stopped at once." "On the contrary," said the middle lodger, "could not Fräulein Samsa come and play in this room, beside us, where it is much more convenient and comfortable?" "Oh certainly," cried Gregor's father, as if he were the violin player. The lodgers came back into the living room and waited. Presently Gregor's father arrived with the music stand, his mother carrying the music and his sister with the violin. His sister quietly made everything ready to start playing; his parents, who had never let rooms before and so had an exaggerated idea of the courtesy due to lodgers, did not venture to sit down on their own chairs; his father leaned against the door, the right hand thrust

angeboten und sass, da sie den Sessel dort liess, wohin ihn
der Herr zufällig gestellt hatte, abseits in einem Winkel.

Die Schwester begann zu spielen; Vater und Mutter verfolgten, jeder von seiner Seite, aufmerksam die Bewegungen
ihrer Hände. Gregor hatte, von dem Spiele angezogen, sich
ein wenig weiter vorgewagt und war schon mit dem Kopf
im Wohnzimmer. Er wunderte sich kaum darüber, dass
er in letzter Zeit so wenig Rücksicht auf die andern nahm;
früher war diese Rücksichtnahme sein Stolz gewesen. Und
dabei hätte er gerade jetzt mehr Grund gehabt, sich zu
verstecken, denn infolge des Staubes, der in seinem Zimmer
überall lag und bei der kleinsten Bewegung umherflog, war
auch er ganz staubbedeckt; Fäden, Haare, Speiseüberrreste
schleppte er auf seinem Rücken und an den Seiten mit sich
herum; seine Gleichgültigkeit gegen alles war viel zu gross,
als dass er sich, wie früher mehrmals während des Tages,
auf den Rücken gelegt und am Teppich gescheuert hätte.
Und trotz dieses Zustandes hatte er keine Scheu, ein Stück
auf dem makellosen Fussboden des Wohnzimmers
vorzurücken.

Allerdings achtete auch niemand auf ihn. Die Familie
war gänzlich vom Violinspiel in Anspruch genommen;
die Zimmerherren dagegen, die zunächst, die Hände in den
Hosentaschen, viel zu nahe hinter dem Notenpult der
Schwester sich aufgestellt hatten, so dass sie alle in die
Noten hätten sehen können, was sicher die Schwester stören
musste, zogen sich bald unter halblauten Gesprächen mit
gesenkten Köpfen zum Fenster zurück, wo sie, vom Vater
besorgt beobachtet, auch blieben. Es hatte nun wirklich
den überdeutlichen Anschein, als wären sie in ihrer An-
nahme, ein schönes oder unterhaltendes Violinspiel zu
hören, enttäuscht, hätten die ganze Vorführung satt und
liessen sich nur aus Höflichkeit noch in ihrer Ruhe stören.
Besonders die Art, wie sie alle aus Nase und Mund den

between two buttons of his livery coat, which was formally buttoned up; but his mother was offered a chair by one of the lodgers and, since she left the chair just where he had happened to put it, sat down in a corner to one side.

Gregor's sister began to play; the father and mother, from either side, intently watched the movements of her hands. Gregor, attracted by the playing, ventured to move forward a little until his head was actually inside the living room. He felt hardly any surprise at his growing lack of consideration for the others; there had been a time when he prided himself on being considerate. And yet just on this occasion he had more reason than ever to hide himself, since owing to the amount of dust which lay thick in his room and rose into the air at the slightest movement, he too was covered with dust; fluff and hair and remnants of food trailed with him, caught on his back and along his sides; his indifference to everything was much too great for him to turn on his back and scrape himself clean on the carpet, as once he had done several times a day. And in spite of his condition, no shame deterred him from advancing a little over the spotless floor of the living room.

To be sure, no one was aware of him. The family was entirely absorbed in the violin playing; the lodgers, however, who first of all had stationed themselves, hands in pockets, much too close behind the music stand so that they could all have read the music, which must have bothered his sister, had soon retreated to the window, half whispering with downbent heads, and stayed there while his father turned an anxious eye on them. Indeed, they were making it more than obvious that they had been disappointed in their expectation of hearing good or enjoyable violin playing, that they had had more than enough of the performance and only out of courtesy suffered a continued disturbance of their peace. From the way they all kept blowing the smoke of their

Rauch ihrer Zigarren in die Höhe bliesen, liess auf grosse
Nervosität schliessen. Und doch spielte die Schwester so
schön. Ihr Gesicht war zur Seite geneigt, prüfend und
traurig folgten ihre Blicke den Notenzeilen. Gregor kroch
noch ein Stück vorwärts und hielt den Kopf eng an den
Boden, um möglicherweise ihren Blicken begegnen zu
können. War er ein Tier, da ihn Musik so ergriff? Ihm war,
als zeige sich ihm der Weg zu der ersehnten unbekannten
Nahrung. Er war entschlossen, bis zur Schwester vorzu-
dringen, sie am Rock zu zupfen und ihr dadurch anzu-
deuten, sie möge doch mit ihrer Violine in sein Zimmer
kommen, denn niemand lohnte hier das Spiel so, wie er es
lohnen wollte. Er wollte sie nicht mehr aus seinem Zimmer
lassen, wenigstens nicht, solange er lebte; seine Schreckge-
stalt sollte ihm zum erstenmal nützlich werden; an allen
Türen seines Zimmers wollte er gleichzeitig sein und den
Angreifern entgegenfauchen; die Schwester aber sollte nicht
gezwungen, sondern freiwillig bei ihm bleiben; sie sollte
neben ihm auf dem Kanapee sitzen, das Ohr zu ihm her-
unterneigen, und er wollte ihr dann anvertrauen, dass er
die feste Absicht gehabt habe, sie auf das Konservatorium
zu schicken, und dass er dies, wenn nicht das Unglück
dazwischen gekommen wäre, vergangene Weihnachten —
Weihnachten war doch wohl schon vorüber? — allen gesagt hätte, ohne sich um irgendwelche Widerreden zu
kümmern. Nach dieser Erklärung würde die Schwester in
Tränen der Rührung ausbrechen, und Gregor würde sich
bis zu ihrer Achsel erheben und ihren Hals küssen, den sie,
seitdem sie ins Geschäft ging, frei ohne Band oder Kragen
trug.

"Herr Samsa!" rief der mittlere Herr dem Vater zu und
zeigte, ohne ein weiteres Wort zu verlieren, mit dem
Zeigefinger auf den langsam sich vorwärtsbewegenden
Gregor. Die Violine verstummte, der mittlere Zimmer-
herr lächelte erst einmal kopfschüttelnd seinen Freunden
zu und sah dann wieder auf Gregor hin. Der Vater schien
es für nötiger zu halten, statt Gregor zu vertreiben, vor-

cigars high in the air through nose and mouth one could divine their irritation. And yet Gregor's sister was playing so beautifully. Her face leaned sideways, intently and sadly her eyes followed the notes of music. Gregor crawled a little farther forward and lowered his head to the ground so that it might be possible for his eyes to meet hers. Was he an animal, that music had such an effect upon him? He felt as if the way were opening before him to the unknown nourishment he craved. He was determined to push forward till he reached his sister, to pull at her skirt and so let her know that she was to come into his room with her violin, for no one here appreciated her playing as he would appreciate it. He would never let her out of his room, at least, not so long as he lived; his frightful appearance would become, for the first time, useful to him; he would watch all the doors of his room at once and spit at intruders; but his sister should need no constraint, she should stay with him of her own free will; she should sit beside him on the sofa, bend down her ear to him and hear him confide that he had had the firm intention of sending her to the Conservatory, and that, but for his mishap, last Christmas—surely Christmas was long past?—he would have announced it to everybody without allowing a single objection. After this confession his sister would be so touched that she would burst into tears, and Gregor would then raise himself to her shoulder and kiss her on the neck, which, now that she went to business, she kept free of any ribbon or collar.

"Mr. Samsa!" cried the middle lodger, to Gregor's father, and pointed, without wasting any more words, at Gregor, now working himself slowly forwards. The violin fell silent, the middle lodger first smiled to his friends with a shake of the head and then looked at Gregor again. Instead of driving Gregor out, his father seemed to think it more needful to begin by soothing

erst die Zimmerherren zu beruhigen, trotzdem diese gar
nicht aufgeregt waren und Gregor sie mehr als das Violinspiel zu unterhalten schien. Er eilte zu ihnen und suchte
sie mit ausgebreiteten Armen in ihr Zimmer zu drängen
und gleichzeitig mit seinem Körper ihnen den Ausblick auf
Gregor zu nehmen. Sie wurden nun tatsächlich ein wenig
böse, man wusste nicht mehr, ob über das Benehmen des
Vaters oder über die ihnen jetzt aufgehende Erkenntnis,
ohne es zu wissen, einen solchen Zimmernachbar wie Gregor besessen zu haben. Sie verlangten vom Vater Erklärungen, hoben ihrerseits die Arme, zupften unruhig an ihren
Bärten und wichen nur langsam gegen ihr Zimmer zurück.
Inzwischen hatte die Schwester die Verlorenheit, in die sie
nach dem plötzlich abgebrochenen Spiel verfallen war,
überwunden, hatte sich, nachdem sie eine Zeitlang in den
lässig hängenden Händen Violine und Bogen gehalten und
weiter, als spiele sie noch, in die Noten gesehen hatte, mit
einem Male aufgerafft, hatte das Instrument auf den Schoss
der Mutter gelegt, die in Atembeschwerden mit heftig ar-
beitenden Lungen noch auf ihrem Sessel sass, und war in
das Nebenzimmer gelaufen, dem sich die Zimmerherren
unter dem Drängen des Vaters schon schneller näherten.
Man sah, wie unter den geübten Händen der Schwester die
Decken und Polster in den Betten in die Höhe flogen und
sich ordneten. Noch ehe die Herren das Zimmer erreicht
hatten, war sie mit dem Aufbetten fertig und schlüpfte
heraus. Der Vater schien wieder von seinem Eigensinn derartig ergriffen, dass er jeden Respekt vergass, den er seinen
Mietern immerhin schuldete. Er drängte nur und drängte,
bis schon in der Tür des Zimmers der mittlere der
Herren donnernd mit dem Fuss aufstampfte und dadurch den Vater zum Stehen brachte. "Ich erkläre hiermit,"
sagte er, hob die Hand und suchte mit den Blicken auch
die Mutter und die Schwester, "dass ich mit Rücksicht auf
die in dieser Wohnung und Familie herrschenden wider-
lichen Verhältnisse" — hiebei spie er kurz entschlossen auf
den Boden — "mein Zimmer augenblicklich kündige. Ich

down the lodgers, although they were not at all agitated and apparently found Gregor more entertaining than the violin playing. He hurried towards them and, spreading out his arms, tried to urge them back into their own room and at the same time to block their view of Gregor. They now began to be really a little angry, one could not tell whether because of the old man's behavior or because it had just dawned on them that all unwittingly they had such a neighbor as Gregor next door. They demanded explanations of his father, they waved their arms like him, tugged uneasily at their beards, and only with reluctance backed towards their room. Meanwhile Gregor's sister, who stood there as if lost when her playing was so abruptly broken off, came to life again, pulled herself together all at once after standing for a while holding violin and bow in nervelessly hanging hands and staring at her music, pushed her violin into the lap of her mother, who was still sitting in her chair fighting asthmatically for breath, and ran into the lodgers' room to which they were now being shepherded by her father rather more quickly than before. One could see the pillows and blankets on the beds flying under her accustomed fingers and being laid in order. Before the lodgers had actually reached their room she had finished making the beds and slipped out. The old man seemed once more to be so possessed by his mulish self-assertiveness that he was forgetting all the respect he should show to his lodgers. He kept driving them on and driving them on until in the very door of the bedroom the middle lodger stamped his foot loudly on the floor and so brought him to a halt. "I beg to announce," said the lodger, lifting one hand and looking also at Gregor's mother and sister, "that because of the disgusting conditions prevailing in this household and family"—here he spat on the floor with emphatic brevity—"I give you notice on the spot. Naturally I won't pay you a penny for the days I have lived here,

werde natürlich auch für die Tage, die ich hier gewohnt habe, nicht das Geringste bezahlen, dagegen werde ich es mir noch überlegen, ob ich nicht mit irgendwelchen — glauben Sie mir — sehr leicht zu begründenden Forderungen gegen Sie auftreten werde." Er schwieg und sah gerade vor sich hin, als erwarte er etwas. Tatsächlich fielen sofort seine zwei Freunde mit den Worten ein: "Auch wir kündigen augenblicklich." Darauf fasste er die Türklinke und schloss mit einem Krach die Tür.

Der Vater wankte mit tastenden Händen zu seinem Sessel und liess sich in ihn fallen; es sah aus, als strecke er sich zu seinem gewöhnlichen Abendschläfchen, aber das starke Nicken seines wie haltlosen Kopfes zeigte, dass er ganz und gar nicht schlief. Gregor war die ganze Zeit still auf dem Platz gelegen, auf dem ihn die Zimmerherren ertappt hatten. Die Enttäuschung über das Misslingen seines Planes, vielleicht aber auch die durch das viele Hungern verursachte Schwäche machten es ihm unmöglich, sich zu bewegen. Er fürchtete mit einer gewissen Bestimmtheit schon für den nächsten Augenblick einen allgemeinen über ihn sich entladenden Zusammensturz und wartete. Nicht einmal die Violine schreckte ihn auf, die, unter den zitternden Fingern der Mutter hervor, ihr vom Schosse fiel und einen hallenden Ton von sich gab.

"Liebe Eltern," sagte die Schwester und schlug zur Einleitung mit der Hand auf den Tisch, "so geht es nicht weiter. Wenn ihr das vielleicht nicht einsehet, ich sehe es ein. Ich will vor diesem Untier nicht den Namen meines Bruders aussprechen und sage daher bloss: wir müssen versuchen, es loszuwerden. Wir haben das Menschenmögliche versucht, es zu pflegen und zu dulden, ich glaube, es kann uns niemand den geringsten Vorwurf machen."

"Sie hat tausendmal recht", sagte der Vater für sich. Die Mutter, die noch immer nicht genug Atem finden konnte, fing mit einem irrsinnigen Ausdruck der Augen dumpf in die vorgehaltene Hand zu husten an.

on the contrary I shall consider bringing an action for damages against you, based on claims—believe me—that will be easily susceptible of proof." He ceased and stared straight in front of him, as if he expected something. In fact his two friends at once rushed into the breach with these words: "And we too give notice on the spot." On that he seized the door-handle and shut the door with a slam.

Gregor's father, groping with his hands, staggered forward and fell into his chair; it looked as if he were stretching himself there for his ordinary evening nap, but the marked jerkings of his head, which was as if uncontrollable, showed that he was far from asleep. Gregor had simply stayed quietly all the time on the spot where the lodgers had espied him. Disappointment at the failure of his plan, perhaps also the weakness arising from extreme hunger, made it impossible for him to move. He feared, with a fair degree of certainty, that at any moment the general tension would discharge itself in a combined attack upon him, and he lay waiting. He did not react even to the noise made by the violin as it fell off his mother's lap from under her trembling fingers and gave out a resonant note.

"My dear parents," said his sister, slapping her hand on the table by way of introduction, "things can't go on like this. Perhaps you don't realize that, but I do. I won't utter my brother's name in the presence of this creature, and so all I say is: we must try to get rid of it. We've tried to look after it and to put up with it as far as is humanly possible, and I don't think anyone could reproach us in the slightest."

"She is more than right," said Gregor's father to himself. His mother, who was still choking for lack of breath, began to cough hollowly into her hand with a wild look in her eyes.

Die Schwester eilte zur Mutter und hielt ihr die Stirn. Der Vater schien durch die Worte der Schwester auf bestimmtere Gedanken gebracht zu sein, hatte sich aufrecht gesetzt, spielte mit seiner Dienermütze zwischen den Tellern, die noch vom Nachtmahl der Zimmerherren her auf dem Tische standen, und sah bisweilen auf den stillen Gregor hin.

"Wir müssen es loszuwerden suchen," sagte die Schwester nun ausschliesslich zum Vater, denn die Mutter hörte in ihrem Husten nichts, "es bringt euch noch beide um, ich sehe es kommen. Wenn man schon so schwer arbeiten muss, wie wir alle, kann man nicht noch zu Hause diese ewige Quälerei ertragen. Ich kann es auch nicht mehr." Und sie brach so heftig in Weinen aus, dass ihre Tränen auf das Gesicht der Mutter niederflossen, von dem sie sie mit mechanischen Handbewegungen wischte.

"Kind," sagte der Vater mitleidig und mit auffallendem Verständnis, "was sollen wir aber tun?"

Die Schwester zuckte nur die Achseln zum Zeichen der Ratlosigkeit, die sie nun während des Weinens im Gegensatz zu ihrer früheren Sicherheit ergriffen hatte.

"Wenn er uns verstünde," sagte der Vater halb fragend; die Schwester schüttelte aus dem Weinen heraus heftig die Hand zum Zeichen, dass daran nicht zu denken sei.

"Wenn er uns verstünde," wiederholte der Vater und nahm durch Schliessen der Augen die Überzeugung der Schwester von der Unmöglichkeit dessen in sich auf, "dann wäre vielleicht ein Übereinkommen mit ihm möglich. Aber so —"

"Weg muss es," rief die Schwester, "das ist das einzige Mittel, Vater. Du musst bloss den Gedanken loszuwerden suchen, dass es Gregor ist. Dass wir es so lange geglaubt haben, das ist ja unser eigentliches Unglück. Aber wie kann es denn Gregor sein? Wenn es Gregor wäre, er hätte längst eingesehen, dass ein Zusammenleben von Menschen mit einem solchen Tier nicht möglich ist, und wäre freiwillig

His sister rushed over to her and held her forehead. His father's thoughts seemed to have lost their vagueness at Grete's words, he sat more upright, fingering his service cap that lay among the plates still lying on the table from the lodgers' supper, and from time to time looked at the still form of Gregor.

"We must try to get rid of it," his sister now said explicitly to her father, since her mother was coughing too much to hear a word, "it will be the death of both of you, I can see that coming. When one has to work as hard as we do, all of us, one can't stand this continual torment at home on top of it. At least I can't stand it any longer." And she burst into such a passion of sobbing that her tears dropped on her mother's face, where she wiped them off mechanically.

"My dear," said the old man sympathetically, and with evident understanding, "but what can we do?"

Gregor's sister merely shrugged her shoulders to indicate the feeling of helplessness that had now overmastered her during her weeping fit, in contrast to her former confidence.

"If he could understand us," said her father, half questioningly; Grete, still sobbing, vehemently waved a hand to show how unthinkable that was.

"If he could understand us," repeated the old man, shutting his eyes to consider his daughter's conviction that understanding was impossible, "then perhaps we might come to some agreement with him. But as it is—"

"He must go," cried Gregor's sister, "that's the only solution, Father. You must just try to get rid of the idea that this is Gregor. The fact that we've believed it for so long is the root of all our trouble. But how can it be Gregor? If this were Gregor, he would have realized long ago that human beings can't live with such a creature, and he'd have gone away on his own accord.

fortgegangen. Wir hätten dann keinen Bruder, aber könnten
weiter leben und sein Andenken in Ehren halten. So aber
verfolgt uns dieses Tier, vertreibt die Zimmerherren, will
offenbar die ganze Wohnung einnehmen und uns auf der
Gasse übernachten lassen. Sieh nur, Vater," schrie sie plötzlich auf, "er fängt schon wieder an!" Und in einem für
Gregor gänzlich unverständlichen Schrecken verliess die
Schwester sogar die Mutter, stiess sich förmlich von ihrem
Sessel ab, als wollte sie lieber die Mutter opfern, als in
Gregors Nähe bleiben, und eilte hinter den Vater, der,
lediglich durch ihr Benehmen erregt, auch aufstand und
die Arme wie zum Schutze der Schwester vor ihr halb
erhob.

Aber Gregor fiel es doch gar nicht ein, irgend jemandem
und gar seiner Schwester Angst machen zu wollen. Er
hatte bloss angefangen sich umzudrehen, um in sein Zimmer
zurückzuwandern, und das nahm sich allerdings auffallend
aus, da er infolge seines leidenden Zustandes bei den
schwierigen Umdrehungen mit seinem Kopf nachhelfen
musste, den er hierbei viele Male hob und gegen den Boden
schlug. Er hielt inne und sah sich um. Seine gute Absicht
schien erkannt worden zu sein; es war nur ein augenblick-
licher Schrecken gewesen. Nun sahen ihn alle schweigend
und traurig an. Die Mutter lag, die Beine ausgestreckt und
aneinandergedrückt, in ihrem Sessel, die Augen fielen ihr
vor Ermattung fast zu; der Vater und die Schwester sassen
nebeneinander, die Schwester hatte ihre Hand um des
Vaters Hals gelegt.

Nun darf ich mich schon vielleicht umdrehen, dachte
Gregor und begann seine Arbeit wieder. Er konnte das
Schnaufen der Anstrengung nicht unterdrücken und musste
auch hie und da ausruhen. Im übrigen drängte ihn auch
niemand, es war alles ihm selbst überlassen. Als er die Umdrehung vollendet hatte, fing er sofort an, geradeaus zurückzuwandern. Er staunte über die grosse Entfernung, die
ihn von seinem Zimmer trennte, und begriff gar nicht,
wie er bei seiner Schwäche vor kurzer Zeit den gleichen

Then we wouldn't have any brother, but we'd be able to go on living and keep his memory in honor. As it is, this creature persecutes us, drives away our lodgers, obviously wants the whole apartment to himself and would have us all sleep in the gutter. Just look, Father," she shrieked all at once, "he's at it again!" And in an access of panic that was quite incomprehensible to Gregor she even left her mother, literally thrusting the chair from her as if she would rather sacrifice her mother than stay so near to Gregor, and rushed behind her father, who also rose up, being simply upset by her agitation, and half-spread his arms out as if to protect her.

Yet Gregor had not the slightest intention of frightening anyone, far less his sister. He had only begun to turn round in order to crawl back to his room, but it was certainly a startling operation to watch, since because of his disabled condition he could not execute the difficult turning movements except by lifting his head and then bracing it against the floor over and over again. He paused and looked round. His good intentions seemed to have been recognized; the alarm had only been momentary. Now they were all watching him in melancholy silence. His mother lay in her chair, her legs stiffly outstretched and pressed together, her eyes almost closing for sheer weariness; his father and his sister were sitting beside each other, his sister's arm around the old man's neck.

Perhaps I can go on turning round now, thought Gregor, and began his labors again. He could not stop himself from panting with the effort, and had to pause now and then to take breath. Nor did anyone harass him, he was left entirely to himself. When he had completed the turn-round he began at once to crawl straight back. He was amazed at the distance separating him from his room and could not understand how in his weak state he had managed to accomplish the same

Weg, fast ohne es zu merken, zurückgelegt hatte. Immerfort nur auf rasches Kriechen bedacht, achtete er kaum
darauf, dass kein Wort, kein Ausruf seiner Familie ihn
störte. Erst als er schon in der Tür war, wendete er den
Kopf, nicht vollständig, denn er fühlte den Hals steif
werden, immerhin sah er noch, dass sich hinter ihm nichts
verändert hatte, nur die Schwester war aufgestanden. Sein
letzter Blick streifte die Mutter, die nun völlig eingeschlafen
war.

Kaum war er innerhalb seines Zimmers, wurde die Tür
eiligst zugedrückt, festgeriegelt und versperrt. Über den
plötzlichen Lärm hinter sich erschrak Gregor so, dass ihm
die Beinchen einknickten. Es war die Schwester, die sich
so beeilt hatte. Aufrecht war sie schon da gestanden und
hatte gewartet, leichtfüssig war sie dann vorwärtsgesprun-
gen, Gregor hatte sie gar nicht kommen hören, und ein
"Endlich!" rief sie den Eltern zu, während sie den Schlüssel
im Schloss umdrehte.

"Und jetzt?" fragte sich Gregor und sah sich im Dunkeln
um. Er machte bald die Entdeckung, dass er sich nun überhaupt nicht mehr rühren konnte. Er wunderte sich darüber
nicht, eher kam es ihm unnatürlich vor, dass er sich bis
jetzt tatsächlich mit diesen dünnen Beinchen hatte fortbe-
wegen können. Im übrigen fühlte er sich verhältnismässig
behaglich. Er hatte zwar Schmerzen im ganzen Leib, aber
ihm war, als würden sie allmählich schwächer und schwächer und würden schliesslich ganz vergehen. Den verfaulten
Apfel in seinem Rücken und die entzündete Umgebung,
die ganz von weichem Staub bedeckt war, spürte er schon
kaum. An seine Familie dachte er mit Rührung und Liebe
zurück. Seine Meinung darüber, dass er verschwinden
müsse, war womöglich noch entschiedener, als die seiner
Schwester. In diesem Zustand leeren und friedlichen Nach-
denkens blieb er, bis die Turmuhr die dritte Morgenstunde
schlug. Den Anfang des allgemeinen Hellerwerdens draussen
vor dem Fenster erlebte er noch. Dann sank sein Kopf

journey so recently, almost without remarking it. Intent on crawling as fast as possible, he barely noticed that not a single word, not an ejaculation from his family, interfered with his progress. Only when he was already in the doorway did he turn his head round, not completely, for his neck muscles were getting stiff, but enough to see that nothing had changed behind him except that his sister had risen to her feet. His last glance fell on his mother, who was now quite overcome by sleep.

Hardly was he well inside his room when the door was hastily pushed shut, bolted and locked. The sudden noise in his rear startled him so much that his little legs gave beneath him. It was his sister who had shown such haste. She had been standing ready waiting and had made a light spring forward, Gregor had not even heard her coming, and she cried "At last!" to her parents as she turned the key in the lock.

"And what now?" said Gregor to himself, looking round in the darkness. Soon he made the discovery that he was now unable to stir a limb. This did not surprise him, rather it seemed unnatural that he should ever actually have been able to move on these feeble little legs. Otherwise he felt relatively comfortable. True, his whole body was aching, but it seemed that the pain was gradually growing less and would finally pass away. The rotting apple in his back and the inflamed area around it, all covered with soft dust, already hardly troubled him. He thought of his family with tenderness and love. The decision that he must disappear was one that he held to even more strongly than his sister, if that were possible. In this state of vacant and peaceful meditation he remained until the tower clock struck three in the morning. The first broadening of light in the world outside the window entered his consciousness once more. Then his head sank to the floor of its own accord

ohne seinen Willen gänzlich nieder, und aus seinen Nüstern strömte sein letzter Atem schwach hervor.

Als am frühen Morgen die Bedienerin kam — vor lauter Kraft und Eile schlug sie, wie oft man sie auch schon gebeten hatte, das zu vermeiden, alle Türen derartig zu, dass in der ganzen Wohnung von ihrem Kommen an kein ruhiger Schlaf mehr möglich war —, fand sie bei ihrem gewöhnlichen kurzen Besuch an Gregor zuerst nichts Besonderes. Sie dachte, er liege absichtlich so unbeweglich da und spiele den Beleidigten; sie traute ihm allen möglichen Verstand zu. Weil sie zufällig den langen Besen in der Hand hielt, suchte sie mit ihm Gregor von der Tür aus zu kitzeln. Als sich auch da kein Erfolg zeigte, wurde sie ärgerlich und stiess ein wenig in Gregor hinein, und erst als sie ihn ohne jeden Widerstand von seinem Platze geschoben hatte, wurde sie aufmerksam. Als sie bald den wahren Sachverhalt erkannte, machte sie grosse Augen, pfiff vor sich hin, hielt sich aber nicht lange auf, sondern riss die Tür des Schlafzimmers auf und rief mit lauter Stimme in das Dunkel hinein: "Sehen Sie nur mal an, es ist krepiert; da liegt es, ganz und gar krepiert!"

Das Ehepaar Samsa sass im Ehebett aufrecht da und hatte zu tun, den Schrecken über die Bedienerin zu verwinden, ehe es dazu kam, ihre Meldung aufzufassen. Dann aber stiegen Herr und Frau Samsa, jeder auf seiner Seite, eiligst aus dem Bett, Herr Samsa warf die Decke über seine Schultern, Frau Samsa kam nur im Nachthemd hervor; so traten sie in Gregors Zimmer. Inzwischen hatte sich auch die Tür des Wohnzimmers geöffnet, in dem Grete seit dem Einzug der Zimmerherren schlief; sie war völlig angezogen, als hätte sie gar nicht geschlafen, auch ihr bleiches Gesicht schien das zu beweisen. "Tot?" sagte Frau Samsa und sah fragend zur Bedienerin auf, trotzdem sie doch alles selbst prüfen und sogar ohne Prüfung erkennen konnte. "Das will ich meinen", sagte die Bedienerin und

and from his nostrils came the last faint flicker of his breath.

When the charwoman arrived early in the morning—what between her strength and her impatience she slammed all the doors so loudly, never mind how often she had been begged not to do so, that no one in the whole apartment could enjoy any quiet sleep after her arrival—she noticed nothing unusual as she took her customary peep into Gregor's room. She thought he was lying motionless on purpose, pretending to be in the sulks; she credited him with every kind of intelligence. Since she happened to have the long-handled broom in her hand she tried to tickle him up with it from the doorway. When that too produced no reaction she felt provoked and poked at him a little harder, and only when she had pushed him along the floor without meeting any resistance was her attention aroused. It did not take her long to establish the truth of the matter, and her eyes widened, she let out a whistle, yet did not waste much time over it but tore open the door of the Samsas' bedroom and yelled into the darkness at the top of her voice: "Just look at this, it's dead; it's lying here dead and done for!"

Mr. and Mrs. Samsa started up in their double bed and before they realized the nature of the charwoman's announcement had some difficulty in overcoming the shock of it. But then they got out of bed quickly, one on either side, Mr. Samsa throwing a blanket over his shoulders, Mrs. Samsa in nothing but her nightgown; in this array they entered Gregor's room. Meanwhile the door of the living room opened, too, where Grete had been sleeping since the advent of the lodgers; she was completely dressed as if she had not been to bed, which seemed to be confirmed also by the paleness of her face. "Dead?" said Mrs. Samsa, looking questioningly at the charwoman, although she could have investigated for herself, and the fact was obvious enough

stiess zum Beweis Gregors Leiche mit dem Besen noch ein
grosses Stück seitwärts. Frau Samsa machte eine Bewegung,
als wolle sie den Besen zurückhalten, tat es aber nicht.
"Nun," sagte Herr Samsa, "jetzt können wir Gott danken."
Er bekreuzte sich, und die drei Frauen folgten seinem Beispiel. Grete, die kein Auge von der Leiche wendete, sagte:
"Seht nur, wie mager er war. Er hat ja auch schon so lange
Zeit nichts gegessen. So wie die Speisen hereinkamen, sind
sie wieder hinausgekommen." Tatsächlich war Gregors
Körper vollständig flach und trocken, man erkannte das
eigentlich erst jetzt, da er nicht mehr von den Beinchen
gehoben war und auch sonst nichts den Blick ablenkte.

"Komm, Grete, auf ein Weilchen zu uns herein", sagte
Frau Samsa mit einem wehmütigen Lächeln, und Grete
ging, nicht ohne nach der Leiche zurückzusehen, hinter
den Eltern in das Schlafzimmer. Die Bedienerin schloss
die Tür und öffnete gänzlich das Fenster. Trotz des frühen
Morgens war der frischen Luft schon etwas Lauigkeit bei-
gemischt. Es war eben schon Ende März.

Aus ihrem Zimmer traten die drei Zimmerherren und
sahen sich erstaunt nach ihrem Frühstück um; man hatte
sie vergessen. "Wo ist das Frühstück?" fragte der mittlere
der Herren mürrisch die Bedienerin. Diese aber legte den
Finger an den Mund und winkte dann hastig und schweigend den Herren zu, sie möchten in Gregors Zimmer
kommen. Sie kamen auch und standen dann, die Hände in
den Taschen ihrer etwas abgenützten Röckchen, in dem
nun schon ganz hellen Zimmer um Gregors Leiche herum.

Da öffnete sich die Tür des Schlafzimmers, und Herr
Samsa erschien in seiner Livree, an einem Arm seine Frau,
am anderen seine Tochter. Alle waren ein wenig verweint;
Grete drückte bisweilen ihr Gesicht an den Arm des
Vaters.

"Verlassen Sie sofort meine Wohnung!" sagte Herr
Samsa und zeigte auf die Tür, ohne die Frauen von sich
zu lassen. "Wie meinen Sie das?" sagte der mittlere der

without investigation. "I should say so," said the charwoman, proving her words by pushing Gregor's corpse
a long way to one side with her broomstick. Mrs.
Samsa made a movement as if to stop her, but checked
it. "Well," said Mr. Samsa, "now thanks be to God."
He crossed himself, and the three women followed his
example. Grete, whose eyes never left the corpse, said:
"Just see how thin he was. It's such a long time since
he's eaten anything. The food came out again just as
it went in." Indeed, Gregor's body was completely flat
and dry, as could only now be seen when it was no
longer supported by the legs and nothing prevented one
from looking closely at it.

"Come in beside us, Grete, for a little while," said
Mrs. Samsa with a tremulous smile, and Grete, not
without looking back at the corpse, followed her parents into their bedroom. The charwoman shut the door
and opened the window wide. Although it was so early
in the morning a certain softness was perceptible in the
fresh air. After all, it was already the end of March.

The three lodgers emerged from their room and were
surprised to see no breakfast; they had been forgotten.
"Where's our breakfast?" said the middle lodger peev-
ishly to the charwoman. But she put her finger to her
lips and hastily, without a word, indicated by gestures
that they should go into Gregor's room. They did so
and stood, their hands in the pockets of their somewhat
shabby coats, around Gregor's corpse in the room where
it was now fully light.

At that the door of the Samsas' bedroom opened and
Mr. Samsa appeared in his uniform, his wife on one
arm, his daughter on the other. They all looked a little
as if they had been crying; from time to time Grete
hid her face on her father's arm.

"Leave my house at once!" said Mr. Samsa, and
pointed to the door without disengaging himself from
the women. "What do you mean by that?" said the

Herren etwas bestürzt und lächelte süsslich. Die zwei anderen hielten die Hände auf dem Rücken und rieben sie ununterbrochen aneinander, wie in freudiger Erwartung eines grossen Streites, der aber für sie günstig ausfallen musste. "Ich meine es genau so, wie ich es sage", antwortete Herr Samsa und ging in einer Linie mit seinen zwei Begleiterinnen auf den Zimmerherrn zu. Dieser stand zuerst still da und sah zu Boden, als ob sich die Dinge in seinem Kopf zu einer neuen Ordnung zusammenstellten. "Dann gehen wir also", sagte er dann and sah zu Herrn Samsa auf, als verlange er in einer plötzlich ihn überkommenden Demut sogar für diesen Entschluss eine neue Genehmigung. Herr Samsa nickte ihm bloss mehrmals kurz mit grossen Augen zu. Daraufhin ging der Herr tatsächlich sofort mit langen Schritten ins Vorzimmer; seine beiden Freunde hatten schon ein Weilchen lang mit ganz ruhigen Händen aufgehorcht und hüpften ihm jetzt geradezu nach, wie in Angst, Herr Samsa könnte vor ihnen ins Vorzimmer eintreten und die Verbindung mit ihrem Führer stören. Im Vorzimmer nahmen alle drei die Hüte vom Kleiderrechen, zogen ihre Stöcke aus dem Stockbehälter, verbeugten sich stumm und verliessen die Wohnung. In einem, wie sich zeigte, gänzlich unbegründeten Misstrauen trat Herr Samsa mit den zwei Frauen auf den Vorplatz hinaus; an das Geländer gelehnt, sahen sie zu, wie die drei Herren zwar langsam, aber ständig die lange Treppe hinunterstiegen, in jedem Stockwerk in einer bestimmten Biegung des Treppenhauses verschwanden und nach ein paar Augenblicken wieder hervorkamen; je tiefer sie gelangten, desto mehr verlor sich das Interesse der Familie Samsa für sie, und als ihnen entgegen und dann hoch über sie hinweg ein Fleischergeselle mit der Trage auf dem Kopf in stolzer Haltung heraufstieg, verliess bald Herr Samsa mit den Frauen das Geländer, and alle kehrten, wie erleichtert, in ihre Wohnung zurück.

Sie beschlossen, den heutigen Tag zum Ausruhen und Spazierengehen zu verwenden; sie hatten diese Arbeits-

middle lodger, taken somewhat aback, with a feeble
smile. The two others put their hands behind them and
kept rubbing them together, as if in gleeful expectation
of a fine set-to in which they were bound to come off
the winners. "I mean just what I say," answered Mr.
Samsa, and advanced in a straight line with his two
companions towards the lodger. He stood his ground at
first quietly, looking at the floor as if his thoughts were
taking a new pattern in his head. "Then let us go, by
all means," he said, and looked up at Mr. Samsa as if in
a sudden access of humility he were expecting some
renewed sanction for this decision. Mr. Samsa merely
nodded briefly once or twice with staring eyes. Upon
that the lodger really did go with long strides into the
hall, his two friends had been listening and had quite
stopped rubbing their hands for some moments and
now went scuttling after him as if afraid that Mr.
Samsa might get into the hall before them and cut them
off from their leader. In the hall they all three took
their hats from the rack, their sticks from the umbrella
stand, bowed in silence and quitted the apartment. With
a suspiciousness which proved quite unfounded Mr.
Samsa and the two women followed them out to the
landing; leaning over the banister they watched the
three figures slowly but surely going down the long
stairs, vanishing from sight at a certain turn of the staircase on every floor and coming into view again after a
moment or so; the more they dwindled, the more the
Samsa family's interest in them dwindled, and when a
butcher's boy met them and passed them on the stairs
coming up proudly with a tray on his head, Mr. Samsa
and the two women soon left the landing and as if a
burden had been lifted from them went back into their
apartment.

They decided to spend this day in resting and going
for a stroll; they had not only deserved such a respite

unterbrechung nicht nur verdient, sie brauchten sie sogar unbedingt. Und so setzten sie sich zum Tisch und schrieben drei Entschuldigungsbriefe, Herr Samsa an seine Direktion, Frau Samsa an ihren Auftraggeber, und Grete an ihren Prinzipal. Während des Schreibens kam die Bedienerin herein, um zu sagen, dass sie fortgehe, denn ihre Morgenarbeit war beendet. Die drei Schreibenden nickten zuerst bloss, ohne aufzuschauen, erst als die Bedienerin sich immer noch nicht entfernen wollte, sah man ärgerlich auf. "Nun?" fragte Herr Samsa. Die Bedienerin stand lächelnd in der Tür, als habe sie der Familie ein grosses Glück zu melden, werde es aber nur dann tun, wenn sie gründlich ausgefragt werde. Die fast aufrechte kleine Straussfeder auf ihrem Hut, über die sich Herr Samsa schon während ihrer ganzen Dienstzeit ärgerte, schwankte leicht nach allen Richtungen. "Also was wollen Sie eigentlich?" fragte Frau Samsa, vor welcher die Bedienerin noch am meisten Respekt hatte. "Ja," antwortete die Bedienerin und konnte vor freundlichem Lachen nicht gleich weiter reden, "also darüber, wie das Zeug von nebenan weggeschafft werden soll, müssen Sie sich keine Sorgen machen. Es ist schon in Ordnung." Frau Samsa und Grete beugten sich zu ihren Briefen nieder, als wollten sie weiterschreiben; Herr Samsa, welcher merkte, dass die Bedienerin nun alles ausführlich zu beschreiben anfangen wollte, wehrte dies mit ausgestreckter Hand entschieden ab. Da sie aber nicht erzählen durfte, erinnerte sie sich an die grosse Eile, die sie hatte, rief offenbar beleidigt: "Adjes allseits", drehte sich wild um und verliess unter fürchterlichem Türezuschlagen die Wohnung.

"Abends wird sie entlassen", sagte Herr Samsa, bekam aber weder von seiner Frau noch von seiner Tochter eine Antwort, denn die Bedienerin schien ihre kaum gewonnene Ruhe wieder gestört zu haben. Sie erhoben sich, gingen zum Fenster und blieben dort, sich umschlungen haltend. Herr Samsa drehte sich in seinem Sessel nach ihnen um und beobachtete sie still ein Weilchen. Dann rief er: "Also

from work, but absolutely needed it. And so they sat down at the table and wrote three notes of excuse, Mr. Samsa to his board of management, Mrs. Samsa to her employer and Grete to the head of her firm. While they were writing, the charwoman came in to say that she was going now, since her morning's work was finished. At first they only nodded without looking up, but as she kept hovering there they eyed her irritably. "Well?" said Mr. Samsa. The charwoman stood grinning in the doorway as if she had good news to impart to the family but meant not to say a word unless properly questioned. The small ostrich feather standing upright on her hat, which had annoyed Mr. Samsa ever since she was engaged, was waving gaily in all directions. "Well, what is it then?" asked Mrs. Samsa, who obtained more respect from the charwoman than the others. "Oh," said the charwoman, giggling so amiably that she could not at once continue, "just this, you don't need to bother about how to get rid of the thing next door. It's been seen to already." Mrs. Samsa and Grete bent over their letters again, as if preoccupied; Mr. Samsa, who perceived that she was eager to begin describing it all in detail, stopped her with a decisive hand. But since she was not allowed to tell her story, she remembered the great hurry she was in, being obviously deeply huffed: "Bye, everybody," she said, whirling off violently, and departed with a frightful slamming of doors.

"She'll be given notice tonight," said Mr. Samsa, but neither from his wife nor his daughter did he get any answer, for the charwoman seemed to have shattered again the composure they had barely achieved. They rose, went to the window and stayed there, clasping each other tight. Mr. Samsa turned in his chair to look at them and quietly observed them for a little. Then he

kommt doch her. Lasst schon endlich die alten Sachen. Und nehmt auch ein wenig Rücksicht auf mich." Gleich folgten ihm die Frauen, eilten zu ihm, liebkosten ihn und beendeten rasch ihre Briefe.

Dann verliessen alle drei gemeinschaftlich die Wohnung, was sie schon seit Monaten nicht getan hatten, und fuhren mit der Elektrischen ins Freie vor die Stadt. Der Wagen, in dem sie allein sassen, war ganz von warmer Sonne durchschienen. Sie besprachen, bequem auf ihren Sitzen zurückgelehnt, die Aussichten für die Zukunft, und es fand sich, dass diese bei näherer Betrachtung durchaus nicht schlecht waren, denn aller drei Anstellungen waren, worüber sie einander eigentlich noch gar nicht ausgefragt hatten, überaus günstig und besonders für später vielversprechend. Die grösste augenblickliche Besserung der Lage musste sich natürlich leicht durch einen Wohnungswechsel ergeben; sie wollten nun eine kleinere und billigere, aber besser gelegene und überhaupt praktischere Wohnung nehmen, als es die jetzige, noch von Gregor ausgesuchte war. Während sie sich so unterhielten, fiel es Herrn und Frau Samsa im Anblick ihrer immer lebhafter werdenden Tochter fast gleichzeitig ein, wie sie in der letzten Zeit trotz aller Plage, die ihre Wangen bleich gemacht hatte, zu einem schönen und üppigen Mädchen aufgeblüht war. Stiller werdend und fast unbewusst durch Blicke sich verständigend, dachten sie daran, dass es nun Zeit sein werde, auch einen braven Mann für sie zu suchen. Und es war ihnen wie eine Bestätigung ihrer neuen Träume und guten Absichten, als am Ziele ihrer Fahrt die Tochter als erste sich erhob und ihren jungen Körper dehnte.

called out: "Come along, now, do. Let bygones be by-gones. And you might have some consideration for me." The two of them complied at once, hastened to him, caressed him and quickly finished their letters.

Then they all three left the apartment together, which was more than they had done for months, and went by tram into the open country outside the town. The tram, in which they were the only passengers, was filled with warm sunshine. Leaning comfortably back in their seats they canvassed their prospects for the future, and it appeared on closer inspection that these were not at all bad, for the jobs they had got, which so far they had never really discussed with each other, were all three admirable and likely to lead to better things later on. The greatest immediate improvement in their condition would of course arise from moving to another house; they wanted to take a smaller and cheaper but also bet-ter situated and more easily run apartment than the one they had, which Gregor had selected. While they were thus conversing, it struck both Mr. and Mrs. Samsa, almost at the same moment, as they became aware of their daughter's increasing vivacity, that in spite of all the sorrow of recent times, which had made her cheeks pale, she had bloomed into a pretty girl with a good figure. They grew quieter and half unconsciously ex-changed glances of complete agreement, having come to the conclusion that it would soon be time to find a good husband for her. And it was like a confirmation of their new dreams and excellent intentions that at the end of their journey their daughter sprang to her feet first and stretched her young body.